Into the Water, Into the Flame

By

Matthew Roy Davey

For H B Stanley

Chapter 1

Prologue: Ten Years Later

The night was still and very dark, a lonely darkness untainted by street lamps or shop lights. Nothing moved or made a sound, it was as though the creatures of the night knew something strange was afoot and were holding their breath. Through skeletal trees and scudding clouds the cold blue of the winter moon cast brittle shadows. Snaking through the loamy soil, a thin stream trickled and gurgled in the silence. A narrow path ran along the edge of the stream, a flattened line of grass rarely trodden, but in the wetness of the soil were footprints leading upstream. They followed the water until the woodland gave way, the trees stopping abruptly in the face of a wall that loomed as tall as a tower block, filling the valley through which the river wound.

From a concrete-lined sluice near the base of the wall, a steady flow of water emerged, falling into a pool where it bubbled and foamed before overflowing and becoming the stream. Beyond the wall, hundreds of thousands of gallons of murky water hung in the dammed valley, dark depths, weed strewn and treacherous, pressing against the obstruction.

From the darkness of the sluice came scraping sounds. A man emerged from the round opening, soaking wet and breathing hard. He dangled his legs over the edge of the pipe's opening and then pushed himself off, landing with a splash in the pool. In his left hand he held a reel of cable which trailed back into the darkness. Reaching up to the outer rim of the sluice he found a small black plastic box with a switch on its surface. Carefully he attached the cable in his hand to an opening in the back of the box.

The man was dressed in black combat trousers, a black polo neck and army boots. On his back he wore a dark, waterproof knapsack. His clothes shone in the moonlight where the water had soaked in, clinging to his thin muscular body.

Pausing for a moment he looked to the star scattered sky. A section was obscured by a strip of blackness, unmarked by the glittering pin pricks, a wooden bridge supported at either end by tall towers. The valley that the bridge traversed was narrow, no more than forty feet wide, but it had steep sides. It would have been beautiful if it had not been amputated, blocked by the huge dam from which the man had climbed.

He splashed through the pool, unconcerned by the noise, and stepped onto the bank. He settled, took one look up at the wall, and then flicked the switch.

From deep within came a concussion, a rumble spreading out in a wave and shaking the earth. There was the briefest moment of silence and then came the sound, a deep throated roar of anger. The earth jolted, shook, and a burst of dust exploded from the sluice, followed by a gout of water that spewed into the pool.

All became still, as before, the stream trickling and gurgling.

It was as though nothing had happened.

The man remained motionless. From deep within the wall came a tearing sound, slow and agonised. A bulge appeared high on the face of the dam, the stonework crazing and cracking.

The man scrambled to his feet and started to run.

Chapter 2

The Darkest Hour

It had been Mike's idea and he had kept reminding Joe of the fact until things started to go wrong, then it had gone from being 'my' plan to 'our' plan. That was typical of Mike, Joe thought, always taking the credit, never taking the blame. They were both in real trouble but despite being more scared than he had ever been in his life, Joe was amazed to find that he still had enough room in his quavering heart to feel annoyed with his best friend.

It had still been dark when they had set out that morning. Joe had pedalled through the silent town, his long legs clad in the cut off Levis that he thought made him look a bit French. His Nike trainers, flashes of white in the darkness, pumped away, turning the pedals, his tyres whirring on the cold tarmac of the road.

The air was chilly, pure and motionless, he saw a cat run across the road and a light go on in an upstairs window but apart from that it was as if he was cycling through a ghost town. He had never been up so early before and was enjoying the eerie stillness of the chilly black morning. The moon hung above him, its white luminosity bathing the town in a frigid light. The sky was clear and the stars glittered more brightly than Joe had ever seen before. It was so beautiful he shivered.

Joe's dad had always been promising to take him out into the countryside to see 'real darkness', darkness where you couldn't see your hand in front of your face. Joe's dad was from the west coast of Scotland, miles from anywhere, where it got *really* dark.

It was from his dad and from Scotland that Joe got his red hair, pale skin and freckles. Joe loved his dad and his dad always meant what he said, it was just that he didn't often to get around to doing what he had promised to do. Joe had still never seen real darkness despite his dad making the promise over a year ago.

As Joe pedalled around the corner of Castle Street and Vicarage Lane he was disappointed to see that Mike was already outside the church where they had arranged to meet. He was sitting on the churchyard wall, blowing into his hands to keep warm. He was wearing jeans and a maroon sweatshirt with a small Lonsdale logo over the heart. A blue woolly hat was jammed on his head from under which bubbled the curls of his sun streaked blond hair. It wasn't that Mike wanted it long, it was just that it

9

wasn't cut very often. Mike's mother said that she had better things to spend her money on than a hair cut. She said that it did him a favour by covering his face, but she only said that because she knew that Mike was really quite handsome and could take a few insults about his appearance, or so she thought.

Unlike Joe, Mike never wore a bike helmet, he said that he wasn't a nerd and that he was too cool for a helmet.

"Yeah, you'll look really cool with brain damage, soup dribbling out of the corner of your mouth," Joe had retorted.

The two boys were always mocking each other but neither one took it seriously. They knew it was almost always a joke, and when it wasn't, well, then they really knew it wasn't.

When he saw Joe approaching, Mike waved and leant across to where his bike was propped against the church wall. He rang his bell as though worried Joe might not see him in the dark.

"Told you I'd get here before you," he called. His voice had only broken a few months before and had a slightly awkward deepness to it like a man who is wearing a coat he's not sure fits properly, tugging at its sleeves and shrugging his shoulders, unsure of how it's hanging on him, worried that he might look foolish.

Joe's voice had broken when he was eleven years old and now he sounded like a man; he was often mistaken for one on the phone, something he took pleasure in without admitting it. He was also one of the only boys in the year that had to shave every day. All Mike could manage was wispy blond fluff across his upper lip.

Joe grunted at Mike, annoyed but trying to hide the fact. It was five minutes before they'd agreed to meet and Joe had been certain that he'd get there first.

It was always the way, somehow, whatever they did, Mike always came out on top; he got better results in tests, he scored higher on computer games, he got in the funny comment that made everyone laugh before Joe even had a chance to begin thinking about what might be funny in a situation. Mike was sharp. Try as he might, Joe couldn't think of one thing that he could do better, other than grow facial hair, and girls weren't impressed with that. Mike was even better looking; the girls gave Mike pearly smiles, giggled at his jokes and flirted. Amy Baird, who Joe liked most out of all the girls in Year 9, flushed an alarming scarlet whenever Mike talked to her. Mike had the sort of hair that all the girls wanted to touch. Joe's hair was curly too, but, of course, it was a deep Scottish auburn – kids called him 'Ginge' when they wanted to be cruel – and Joe kept it cut short to stop it growing as it did, upwards and outwards in an afro style, not like Mike's which flowed down in casual waves and made him look like a surfer.

To someone who didn't know any better it might seem that Mike had it all. Joe knew better, he knew that Mike *didn't* have it all, far from it. Hardly anybody at school knew, but there were things in Mike Werneria's life that no one would want in theirs.

As he had ridden up to Mike, Joe had been glad to see that he wasn't smoking. Sometimes Mike would steal them from his dad's jacket and try to get Joe to try one but Joe had always resisted so far. 'You'll look cool with cancer,' he'd say to Mike. Mike was always more interested in looking good than thinking about his safety or his future, he didn't seem capable of looking more than a day ahead. It was what made him fun, but it was also what made him a little dangerous, both to himself and others around him.

Dawn's first light was beginning to bleed out across the darkness of the sky. The sun was just beginning to crest the distant hills. It was amazing how quickly it had gone from moon-lit darkness to a pale half-light. The birds were beginning to sing in an ecstasy of chirping.

"Did you bring a jacket?" Joe asked, pointing up at the red clouds on the eastern horizon.

Mike's gaze followed Joe's finger up to the sky.

"Yeah," he replied, shrugging. "Why?"

"Red sky in the morning, shepherd's warning. It's going to rain."

"Is it bollocks," Mike scoffed. "The man on the news last night said it would be sunny all day."

Joe thought that perhaps the clouds were warning them about something else, something worse, but it seemed a stupid thought so he didn't say it, even as a joke. Joe's jokes didn't always come off, unlike Mike's. Instead he pointed towards Mike's bike.

"Come on then," he said. "Let's go. We've twenty five miles to do before ten o'clock."

Mike jumped off the wall and moved to his bike, slinging his bag across his broad, muscular shoulders as he did so. He saddled up, brought his bike around level with Joe's and then with a crunch of gravel they moved out into the road. Both of them rose from their saddles and pumped at their pedals, quickly picking up speed, racing one another, neither one wanting to be second.

Within ten minutes they had passed the last of the housing estates and The Royal George pub that marked the edge of town and were on the main road, the road that led to their distant destination. As the sun climbed slowly into the summer sky they chattered about the coming day.

Little did they know that before very long they would both be praying that they would live to see another.

Chapter 3

The Plan

Mike Werneria was of the opinion that Stonebridge was the most boring town in Britain. In fact, he often said, if London was the head of Britain then Stonebridge was the arsehole.

Joe didn't agree, he quite liked Stonebridge, even if it was a bit sleepy and boring. It gave them the chance to make things up for themselves, nothing was laid on for them like it was for city kids. 'Nothing's going to happen if you don't make it happen. If you don't like the news, go out and make your own,' Joe's dad often said whenever Joe had complained about being bored, and he should know, coming from the remote part of Scotland that he did.

A river ran sleepily through what used to be the centre of Stonebridge and then under the old mill. There the steadily moving weight of the water drove the paddles of the big wheel that had driven the mechanism inside the building. Inside the machinery helped in the manufacture of paper products that the Frayne family who owned the mill had packaged up and delivered to stationers across the country. In fact the river still drove the big wheel, it just didn't drive anything inside anymore; the mill had closed down many years before and the mechanism had been disengaged so that the wheel revolved pointlessly, a picturesque diversion for the few tourists who passed through the town.

Nowadays the people who lived in Stonebridge commuted to the nearest big city or worked in the slaughterhouse or the industrial estate on the edge of town. There was very little work in the town itself, just the supermarket and the few remaining independent shops.

Apart from the old High Street, which looked like something from a postcard Stonebridge was little more than a housing estate with a couple of pubs and the occasional rank of shops. There was no cinema, no bowling alley and no burger bars, all there was, was an expensive sports centre and a park with two tatty old swings, a climbing frame and a slide that your jeans stuck to half way down.

It *was* quite boring Joe had to admit when he thought about it, even if you did have an imagination. Of course boredom and imagination weren't always a good combination and Joe and Mike had often got themselves into trouble in the pursuit of amusement.

Stonebridge was just big enough to have its own secondary school, Millfields, and that was where Joe and Mike went. They were both in the same Year 9 tutor group and it had been during a particularly boring English lesson with Mr Quinte that the big idea had been born.

Mr Quinte had been droning on about angels when Mike had leaned over and whispered into Joe's ear. He then shoved the leaflet that had dropped through his letter box the previous evening across the desk. Joe recognised it immediately, he had received the same one on his own door mat. The boys mistakenly assumed that the leaflet was a part of an advertising campaign and that everyone had received one.

What neither boy had realised was that they were the only people in the town to have received the leaflet.

As soon as Mike had announced his plan Joe had agreed, it was incredible, audacious and a little dangerous. They would certainly be in a lot of trouble if their parents ever found out, but nevertheless, Joe was never in any doubt that they should do it and do it as soon as possible.

The long summer holiday was only a week away and so while Mr Quinte blathered on about some islands off the coast of Ireland, Joe and Mike made notes in the backs of their books about what they needed to do to get their plan to work.

By the time the school day was over it was agreed, they would each tell their parents that they were going camping with a third friend, Billy Fisher, who was actually away on holiday in America for a month. If their parents tried phoning Billy's parents, which they wouldn't because they didn't know them - Billy had only moved into the area at Christmas - there would be no reply and so they would phone the other boy's parents who would confirm the story, or at least what they knew of it.

It was genius, a genius plan, dreamt up by a genius, Mike had said. Joe had just grunted but he was certainly excited about the prospect of what lay in store.

And so it was when they shut their front doors behind them - their parents safely in bed and still asleep, not realising that their boys were leaving on their 'camping trip' so early – that Mike and Joe headed off on what they thought would be a journey of fun and adventure, but in fact, would turn out to be a journey into terror.

Chapter 4

The watcher

Somewhere, not so very far away from Stonebridge, sat a man on a chair in a cold lonely room. His head was bald but for wild greying hair at the back and sides that stood out from his narrow skull. His crooked eyebrows bushed out in crazed tangles over his flinty grey eyes.

On a wooden table in front of him was a bowl carved from the trunk of a tree that had died over two hundred years ago. In the bowl was water, pure clear water, but water that had been drawn from a special source, a source unlike any other.

The man gazed into the bowl and beneath the gently rippling surface of the water strange images moved as though emerging from the darkness of the wood, tricks of the light in the shifting of the liquid.

Only these weren't tricks of the light and there was nothing in the water at all. Something was there though, images, but images that only the man could see, images that came from a place that only few could summon.

Had anyone else peered over the man's shoulder at that moment they should have wondered why he was staring into a wooden bowl filled to the brim with nothing but water.

The man chuckled, a low mirthless sound, a sound not of joy but of satisfaction.

He had been watching them, watching the two of them for a long time, ever since they had visited the year before. Time had passed and all the while he had been planning, plotting a way to conjure them into his web. When he was ready he put his plans into action and in the ancient bowl he had watched them receive the information that he had sent in the post.

The invitation to come and join him.

Not that they had known that it was an invitation when they had received it. It had seemed like an ordinary leaflet advertising an attraction.

Nothing was clear to these boys, they had no idea what was happening, of the plans that were being drawn against them.

It hadn't mattered that the boys didn't realise that it wasn't an invitation, they had received it, they had read it, and now they were coming.

The man laughed again, a pitiless sound like winter rain running down a storm drain.

Under deeper water, much deeper water, so deep that the light barely filtered through the floating algae, something moved. Something large and very old. It shifted its bulk and sent up a cloud of silt and organic matter that had floated down through the depths.

The creature hadn't moved in a very long time. It hadn't eaten in a very long time. And now it was hungry.

It opened one eye, a huge yellow eye.

Chapter 5

The Journey

"We'll need to take jumpers. It could get cold in the night," Mike had said earlier that week. He had been lying on Joe's bedroom floor as they had planned their trip. "And we probably won't have any cover."

"Yeah," added Joe. "And if it's warm we can just use our jumpers as a pillow."

Now that they were on the move a thought occurred to Joe, what would they use for pillows if it *wasn't* warm?

Other items in their bags were torches, bottled water, and anoraks. It would be a rough night's sleep without blanket above or mattress beneath but that was how it had to be, where they were going they were going without permission. It gave them both a delicious thrill, the thought of doing something wrong, of getting one over on someone else, of getting something for nothing. And what harm would it be doing anyone? And what was the worst thing that could happen if they did get caught? After all, they could only be thrown out, couldn't they?

It hadn't occurred to either of the boys that getting caught was by no means the worst thing that could happen to them.

The day was opening before them like a blossoming flower, the sky growing lighter and warmer, ripening to an orange glow.

As they cycled on they passed ancient churches, old manor houses, slowly crumbling mile stones, their numbers and names fading with the centuries of wind and rain. Birds darted overhead and mist hung in low valleys as they pedalled along the roads that clung to the edges of the slopes, dipping and rising with the contours of the ancient landscape, the same landscape that the Romans had seen, thought Joe, as he imagined the legions marching across the hills.

It was a tough ride, a lot of hills, but both Mike and Joe were fit. Living in Stonebridge there wasn't much to do so bike riding was something that they found themselves doing a lot.

As the sun climbed higher the numbers of cars on the road increased as people began to make their way to work. The boys found that they had to ride single file, there simply wasn't enough room on the road to ride two abreast, and as a result they were less able to talk. It didn't matter though because as the road got steeper they didn't have the breath to spare.

Mike didn't like silence, he always wanted to fill it with a joke or just some meaningless chatter. Silence meant that he started thinking, and when he started thinking then bad thoughts appeared in his head, thoughts that made him sad and made him angry, thoughts that scared him as well. Whatever was going to be on offer today couldn't scare him, he thought, nothing could be as bad as what he had to live with. Mike wished his family could be like Joe's, Joe's family were so calm, so *boring*.

Joe, on the other hand, was glad his family were boring. As he rode along - behind Mike of course, Mike always had to take the lead - he thought about Mike's dad and how glad he was that his dad didn't get angry like Mike's had, angry over the smallest thing.

Once Joe had called around and Mike had come to the door with red eyes and a bruise on his left cheek. Joe hadn't said anything but later that morning Mike had asked Joe if he thought it was possible to want to kill someone you loved. Joe had been shocked but had covered up his reaction and said that he wasn't sure, maybe if it was to put them out of their misery. Mike had nodded and stared at the ground. Then he had farted and the pair of them had cracked up laughing. Their laughter was relief more than anything else, relief at not having to carry on looking at an ugly truth.

Not long after that - Joe couldn't believe it was only three months ago, it seemed like much more time had passed - Mike's dad had been killed in a car crash. A lorry had skidded in the rain and jack-knifed in front of his car. Joe wondered if Mike felt guilty about what he'd said that day, or if maybe he was just relieved he was gone. It was hard to tell what Mike was thinking at the best of times, but when it came to his dad Joe had even less idea.

Joe and Mike talked about almost everything usually, but for some reason Mike's dad was the one thing they never talked about. It was a subject that sat there like a skeleton propped on the corner of a settee that everyone can see but prefers to ignore, they just avoid sitting in that particular corner. Joe wondered if it might not be better to point out the skeleton and then get it good and buried, but he could never think of how to bring it up. Joe couldn't imagine how awful it would be if one of his own parents died, he didn't even want to think about it. He knew Mike missed his father - ever since he had died he'd worn his dad's gold necklace with its little golden cross - but he also suspected that Mike's life was in many ways better without him around. Joe had thought about Mike's feelings a lot since the accident and he was pretty sure he knew what was going on in his friend's head. He was grieving because he loved his dad, but he was relieved he was gone, almost happy, and for that he felt guilty. Mike seemed so lucky in so many ways - looks, sporting ability, brains - but Joe knew him better, he knew he didn't like himself very much, and now, since his father was dead, he feared that Mike was beginning to hate himself.

By quarter past eight both boys were getting tired and so they pulled off the main road and pedalled their bikes for the quarter of a mile that led into the middle of a village that Mike said he knew. Apparently there was a gunsmiths there and his dad had taken him along on a couple of occasions when he had gone to buy shotgun shells.

The road into the town centre opened up into a huge pie slice of cobble stone where in the past a market would once have taken place, all hustle and bustle of stalls and shouting, but where now white painted rectangles were lined up neatly next to one another to show where cars should park. For now though it was almost empty.

Higgledy-piggledy buildings, all of them built by men long dead, lined each side of the market place. In the middle of the car park was a sand stone column atop of a plinth of steps. Carved into the side were the names of the boys and men who had died in both world wars.

Mike and Joe dismounted and leaned their bikes against the sandstone steps, then took off their bags and sat down, drinking from their water bottles and watching the few cars that went past.

Mike took off his sweatshirt and stuffed it into his bag. He sat there flexing the muscles in his arms and Joe could tell that he had been working out with his brother's weights again. Mike went through stages of body building which would last for a couple of months at a time. He would down protein drinks and his size would increase impressively only to subside again when he gave up and a growth spurt stretched him out and slimmed him down again.

Joe was amused to see that Mike was picking at a spot on his chin that appeared to have been covered with some sort of make up. Despite the temptation to ridicule Mike, Joe decided not to say anything. He didn't want to spoil the pleasant air of excitement and comradeship that he felt between them as they sat there in the cool morning sun.

"Have you noticed Lorraine Abbott?" asked Mike expressionlessly.

Joe laughed into his drink.

"I know. They're getting massive."

"She could do with a new blouse. She's bursting out of the one she's wearing at the moment."

"I know. It's great."

"Imagine what they'll be like at the end of the summer holidays!"

"I know. You should have seen her the other day. She was playing netball and they were flying about all over the place."

"Cool!"

They both laughed and for a moment there was an easy silence between them.

"Isn't it nice to see everyone going to work," said Mike. "And us here, free as birds. They'll be stuck inside, stuck at a desk and staring out of the window while we'll be out having a laugh."

Joe nodded and Mike went on.

"It makes it everything sweeter, I reckon, if you're having fun while other people aren't." He paused, watching a Porsche drive past. "It's like being in prison, having to go to work or going to school."

Mike paused for a moment, contemplating the weight of his own words and Joe realised that it wasn't a good moment to offer his own opinion.

"I want to make loads of money and retire early," Mike went on. "Enjoy life. I'd never get bored. You've just got to have good ideas. Something to spend your money on. Don't you reckon?"

"Yeah," Joe said. "Life could be one long summer holiday."

There was a pause as they drank from their bottles and then Mike spoke again.

"It's like I said, having fun is always better when someone else isn't having it, don't you reckon?"

Joe nodded, squinting into the sun.

"Suppose so. It's a bit sick though, isn't it."

"Yeah," Mike replied and they both laughed.

"You know," said Mike. "If I won the lottery I'd never be bored again in my whole life."

"Obviously," said Joe, shoving a chewing gum into his mouth.

"No," said Mike, shaking his head. He turned to Joe and spoke as though to an idiot. "It's not obvious. You read it about it all the time. It happens all the time. Some knob end wins the lottery and then a year later they're moaning how they're bored and how it's ruining their life."

"'Spose so," conceded Joe, chewing on his gum and watching a woman push a pram on the opposite pavement.

"Moaning, how everyone just wants to be friends with them for their money," Mike went on, fiddling with his spot again.

"I could deal with that."

"No one would be friends with you even if you were a billionaire," said Mike, punching Joe on the arm. Joe punched Mike back a little harder than he had meant to. An elderly man getting out of his car nearby gave them a disapproving glare and they stopped laughing and settled back.

They were quite for a moment, watching the old man, his back straight as a soldier's as he walked slowly and stiffly away.

Mike took a swig from his bottle and went on.

"Seriously though, every day, something different. There's so much to do, so many different things to do in the world. How could you be bored? That's what money's for isn't it? Doing stuff."

Joe nodded.

They sat for a moment in silence drinking their water until, without a word passing between them, they simultaneously capped their bottles and got to their feet. It was as though a moment of telepathy had occurred between them, though neither boy noticed, and if they did they didn't mention it. They shouldered their bags before getting on their bikes and setting off out of the village and back to the main road.

Joe was beginning to worry about what his mum might do if she ever found out about what they were doing. He wasn't so bothered about his dad, his dad was so calm that he was almost asleep half the time. He worked so hard that when he relaxed he was almost comatose, his big red head leaning tilted back on the sofa as he gawped at the television.

His mum though, she was calm most of the time but when she went mad she *really* went mad. Her face would turn crimson and her hair would start flying about everywhere as she snapped and jerked about the room. It was scary. She didn't hit Joe very often but when she did it made his brain shake within his skull; that was one of the things that made it scary, wondering if it was one of the times that he'd get a wallop. The sheer force and intensity of her temper was pretty frightening as well, it was like she was possessed by a demon and it was all focussed on Joe.

Still, most of the time she was alright. It was probably just the stress of Joe's dad being away so much.

At least she was better than Mike's mum.

Joe glanced at his watch, determined to forget about her for now. It was eight twenty seven and according to the schedule they had drawn up in

Joe's bedroom and they were supposed to be an hour and a half away from where they were going.

Joe was pretty sure that they were running late.

Chapter 6

The struggle

The further they went and the closer they got the worse the traffic became, carloads of children and teenagers, coaches packed with excited faces. The vehicles would slow down behind the boys and then wait there, engines idling or impatiently revving and then accelerate with a roar to pass when there was space on the narrow road. They would leave in their wake a cloud of flat metallic fumes that choked the boys as they laboured up a never ending series of never ending gradients.

The sun was fully up now and its heat was already warming the air.

The boys had stopped a couple of miles earlier for Joe to take off his jumper, Mike complaining all the while that he should have taken it off at the war memorial like he had. Joe knew that he was glad of the stop though. Despite their disrobing both boys were sweating profusely, Joe a little more than Mike, and neither of them could spare the breath for a shouted conversation any more.

Joe was wearing a plain white T-shirt, Mike on the other hand had on his prized blue Adidas T-shirt. He was very proud of it and Joe knew that it had cost at least four times as much as his white one had. Joe thought it was a bit daft to spend so much money on a logo.

As the morning wore on Joe was beginning to wonder if the whole idea of the trip had been such a good idea after all, his legs were aching, his jeans were rubbing against his thighs, and his lungs were starting to burn. He would have stopped if it wasn't for the fact that Mike was ahead of him and he could never allow Mike to think that he was somehow fitter or stronger than Joe, even if they both knew that he actually was. He watched the muscles in Mike's calves flexing impressively under the strain of the hill.

Eventually, to Joe's immense relief and secret delight, it was Mike who called for a break. They had just crested a long and torturous hill and were beginning to freewheel down an equally long though not quite so steep slope. The traffic jam that had been building behind them for the last three miles began to whiz past like the air out of a balloon. Almost all of the traffic was going in their direction, very little passed on the other side of the road.

Joe felt sick from the exertion and all he could do was hold up a hand in agreement when Mike looked back and pointed to an old sand stone building that lay several hundred yards down the road in the bottom of the valley. Words were beyond Joe; he hoped he'd catch his breath before they got to the foot of the hill and he had to talk to Mike. Pride was everything in situations like these.

The spokes whirred and the wind whistled in the boys' ears as they enjoyed the cool air rushing in their faces and filling their burning lungs. At the bottom of the slope the boys freewheeled into the forecourt of what turned out to be a disused railway station.

The main building had a sign outside it saying 'Betty's Tearoom' but another sign in the door that said 'Closed'. It was still too early.

The boys parked their bikes up against the wall and without saying a word, removed their bags from their sweaty backs and took long drinks. By the time they had finished, both bottles were empty and both boys were gasping.

"Going to have to get these filled up somewhere," said Mike.

Joe nodded.

"Let's have a look around," Mike went on. "See if we can find someone. See if we can find a tap."

They walked around the outside of the building but everywhere was deserted and there was no sign of a tap. All they could hear was the constant sound of traffic on the main road.

On the other side of the station building was a platform and then a three foot drop to the old track bed. It had been concreted over and looked like it was used as a cycle track. Off to the left the tree lined path went under a bridge and then curved away to the right. Off to their right, after a couple of hundred yards, the track disappeared into a tunnel that burrowed into the side of the hill they had just traversed. Orange lights illuminated the way, disappearing into the darkening gloom of a far off bend.

"Bloody hell, Mike!" spat Joe as he saw the tunnel. "I bet we could have come along that way and then we could have saved ourselves all that climbing."

"Yeah, but where does it go?" asked Mike defensively. Neither of them knew where it went. It could be that it emerged at the far side of the hill in a place far from where they'd been coming from. Still there was a note of unease in Mike's voice, he had planned the route and he hadn't realised that there was a cycle track.

"Don't get snotty with me, anyway," Mike continued. "You could have got off your backside and done some of the planning and then *you* might have found this route."

"I'm not being snotty with you," said Joe. "I'm just saying, that's all." He sounded sulky and he knew it.

There was silence between them for a moment.

"Don't know why they don't put tracks down again," said Joe, trying to smooth away the memory of their disagreement. "Listen to the racket all those cars and coaches make. They could get rid of half of them if there was a train running."

They were silent again, listening to the growls and roars of the passing vehicles. All of a sudden it became quiet, a sudden absence of traffic, no cars or coaches on the road, a slice of half silence around them, only the sounds of birds and the wind and something else, distant and almost indefinable.

With a sudden flash of movement, Mike jumped to his feet.

"Can you hear that?"

Joe nodded. He'd heard it too and realised what the distant noise was, it was the sound, far off, of screaming.

"That's people on a ride," shouted Mike. "We must be nearly there."

Joe clambered to his feet a smile spreading slowly across his face. Now there wouldn't be any more hills, or many more at least.

"Come on!" said Mike. "Let's go. We can get a drink when we get there. It'll only take ten minutes, I reckon."

Joe's phone rang, a harsh electronic jangle from inside his jeans. The two boys looked at each other with blank expressions.

"Well," said Mike. "Aren't you going to answer it? Who is it?"

Joe took the mobile from his pocket and peered at the screen.

"It's my mum. I didn't think we'd get any reception out here."

"You'd better answer it," said Mike. "There's no noise here apart from the traffic. You can tell her that you're in a service station or something. She won't guess."

"Good idea," replied Joe and pressed answer.

"Hullo?" he said. "Mum?" There was silence for a moment as Joe listened, his face frowning in concentration. "Yeah." Another pause. "Umm, yeah, it's fine." Pause. "Alright." And then in an embarrassed and hasty mutter. "Love you too. Bye." Joe turned the phone off, his face red.

Mike wasn't going to let his friend get away without a little teasing.

"How sweet! What a good little boy you are." He punched Joe softly on the arm and blew a big wet kiss in the air. "MMMWAH!"

Secretly Mike wished that was how he signed off when he spoke to *his* mum. Mike's mother never said that sort of thing to him. Not anymore. Mike knew that it was pretty unlikely that his mum would even bother phoning him to see if he was okay.

"Up yours," Joe grunted. Although he was embarrassed he knew exactly what Mike would be thinking.

"Did she believe you?"

"Yeah, think so."

"Excellent," said Mike, clapping his hands together. "Come on then, what are we waiting for? The gates are open, the rides are rolling and we're outside. Let's *go*."

They mounted up and set off. Joe was still frowning. Something was wrong, he was sure, but he couldn't put his finger on what it was.

After half a mile of slow, steady and painful uphill riding they came to a turning off the main road, a wide driveway that led through huge black wrought iron gates. Coach after coach and car after car was filing slowly through the gates under an enormous black and red sign that read,

Welcome to

Terror Hall

You'll be screaming – for more

"We did it!" Mike shouted. They pulled over to the side of the driveway, right underneath the sign. Mike slapped Joe on the back. Despite his misgivings Joe felt a grin spreading across his face. It was quite an achievement, twenty five miles across hill and dale and all before ten thirty in the morning. They were ahead of schedule and they had done it right under the noses of their unsuspecting parents.

But Joe didn't want to think about that. It was at that point that he realised what it was that was making him feel uncomfortable, he didn't like lying to his mum.

There was a blast of horn right behind them. They both jumped so much they almost lost their balance and fell off their bikes.

"Move your bloomin' arses," yelled a red faced coach driver, missing them by inches as he drove past.

"Up yours, Granddad," yelled Mike and stuck two fingers up. The bus driver stuck his own two fingers out of the window to return the gesture.

"I hope we don't see him when we get inside," muttered Joe.

"Well then, let's get our arses moving, like the gentleman said," grinned Mike.

The boys followed the flow of traffic as it wound its way down the long driveway, and then turned off into a large area marked 'Coach Parking'.

They lifted their bikes over a metal fence in the farthest corner of the coach park and then chained them to the railings. Then, carefully, they pulled on the lowest branches of an overhanging tree until the bikes were almost entirely concealed. They didn't want the bikes to be discovered after all the coaches and cars had been driven away that night, that might threaten their plan.

From somewhere not so far away came the rattle and roar of a rollercoaster careering along and down the tracks of a nearby ride, and over that screams of delight pierced the morning air as riders were plunged from heights to depths and then rocketed back up again. The noise of the machinery, the speeding metal wheels on the metal of the track and the screams from the bodies inside sent ripples of excitement up the boys' backs.

Once the bikes had been safely stowed Mike and Joe began to run towards the turnstiles, desperate to get inside and experience the rides that they had been talking about for the past month.

During that time, every penny of every bit of pocket money they had been given or earned from doing chores had been squirreled away ready to pay for that precious one day ticket which they would only be able to afford once a year. Mike had also made a little bit from pilfering and petty thefts, but he had shame enough to keep that from Joe. He didn't want Joe thinking that he wasn't as good at earning money as he was.

Joe, however, knew the truth, he wasn't stupid. He could see the look in Mike's eye when the teacher interrogated the class after something went missing from someone's bag, or he would see Mike doing something in the corner of a room, trying to conceal the fact that he was counting money. He didn't know how Mike could do that. He knew that it was wrong to steal, especially from individuals; that was even worse than stealing from shops, and Mike did that too. It was Mike's biggest weakness, he was a thief, but every time Joe tried to bring it up with him it blew up into a huge row. It was best just to leave it and hope that one day Mike saw sense and turned honest. Joe didn't hold out much hope though.

As they reached the path at the end of the coach park Joe reflected on the fact that it was a good thing that they had a plan, a plan to beat the system of Terror Hall. Otherwise the money that they were about to pay would have seemed awfully expensive for just one day's fun.

Back in the coach park, in the tree above the bicycles, a crow watched the boys as they disappeared towards the entrance. There was something in its eyes, a twinkle of intelligence in the dark pools of its beady round irises that was different from other birds, unusual, unsettling. It gathered itself up and shook its body with a clattering rattle of feathers before coughing up a low cackle. Slowly, as though winding itself up, it began to beat its wings, slapping them together like bits of old tarpaulin, until it rose slowly up into the perfect arc of blue sky.

Chapter 7

Crossing the Threshold

They had first thought of scaling a wall or cutting through the perimeter fence with wire cutters, but Mike's older brother, Stevie - a rogue and a crook if ever there was one, but one who was always good to Mike and Joe - had said that he and his mates had tried it once before and it hadn't worked.

Stevie was actually Mike's half- brother from their mother's previous marriage. That marriage hadn't lasted long though and Stevie's dad had done a runner when he was still very young. He had taken Mike's dad's name and so was also a Werneria.

Stevie had told of how they'd driven up in one of his mates' cars, a gentleman by the nickname of Spud who had owned a battered Ford Mondeo. Once parked in the visitors' car park the three young men had started looking for a way in. What they'd found was barbed wire, electrified fences, cameras and guards with dogs who'd told them to push off round to the front and pay just like everyone else. Stevie, Spud, and the third member of Stevie's musketeer gang, Wang, who wasn't Chinese and didn't even look remotely Chinese, had been forced to retreat back to the car defeated, and from there they'd taken the long and humiliating drive home. They'd been so confident that they'd get in without paying that they hadn't brought enough money to pay if things went wrong.

Mike and Joe weren't going to make that mistake. They had enough money to get in and their plan only went into action once they were actually inside the theme park.

They'd both been there once before, the previous year. It had been a school trip and they'd had a brilliant day charging around with their friends, shouting out where they should go next, which ride was closest, which would be best, which would have the shortest queues. They'd had so much fun to squeeze into one short day - too much fun to squeeze into one short day as it turned out - that when the time came for them to leave they had to do so without going on at least three of the rides they'd been planning to.

The strange thing about that visit, Joe remembered, was that he'd felt as though he was being watched, a burning sensation that followed him all day. He'd kept looking around but hadn't been able to spot anyone spying on him or even any cameras. Eventually he'd put it down to paranoia. He'd not mentioned it to Mike, although if he had he would have discovered that Mike had felt the same eerie sensation all day.

Anyway, they weren't going to be short of time on this trip, no, they would have plenty of time this time. One of the features of Terror Hall - a feature usually ignored by the children and teenagers, but often appreciated by older visitors looking to put their feet up and escape the hubbub for half an hour – were the extensive and elaborate gardens that stretched out across several acres of the theme park. Paths crisscrossed the area, opening out onto ponds, walled gardens, pagodas and lawns. The paths themselves were bordered with bushes and plants from all over the world.

Terror Hall had been built on the site of a stately home owned by an ancient and wealthy family. Two hundred years ago a member of the family had decided to impress his guests by planting out a garden that would be the envy of Europe. He had gone about the task with dedication and lavish spending, succeeding in creating a garden that was considered so important that the developers weren't allowed to touch it when the estate became a theme park.

It was on the trip with the school that it had occurred to Mike that the gardens were so large and the foliage so dense that it should be easy to hide out in them over night and thus be able to wake the next day undetected and sneak out to enjoy Terror Hall for two days instead of one. They wouldn't re-enter the park the following day, they would simply never leave!

What they would do, the boys decided, was leave their bags in one of the lockers that were provided near the entrance of the park and then pick them up at the end of the day; the last ride was at 5 thirty and chucking out time was 6 o'clock but they would pick the bags up a little earlier, just to make sure that they were able to lose themselves in the crowds without any of the park employees noticing that they were going in the wrong direction, away from the gates and towards the gardens. Once in the gardens they would make their way to a place where they would bunk down for the night, somewhere secluded, off from any of the main paths, somewhere sheltered and reasonably comfortable, somewhere they would have scouted earlier during the day. They would have to lie low for a while as it would be early and there might be guards checking to make sure no-one was doing exactly what it was they were planning on doing.

"What if they have dogs?" Joe had wondered. He'd had a mortal fear of dogs ever since one had bitten him when he was seven years old.

Mike had a solution to the problem of the dogs, some sort of spray that his brother Stevie had that put dogs off the scent. Quite what Stevie would have needed this spray for was anyone's guess, it was almost certainly illegal, but he had it and he claimed it worked, and that was all that mattered. Mike would steal it out of his brother's bedroom and replace it when they got home from their adventure, if there was any left, of course. When they were in the relevant part of the garden they would spray the area where they had left the path and also around wherever it was they were going to bivouac.

Once it got dark and once all the theme park workers went home they could even explore the park in darkness. How cool would that be? What a plan! What could possibly go wrong?

Chapter 8

Thrill Seeking

Just inside the entrance were rows of bright orange metal lockers. The boys selected one each and stashed their bags, jumpers and coats.

While they queued at the turnstiles the boys had decided they would go on a couple of rides before they started looking for a good place to doss down for the night. To do something as mundane as finding a hiding place when there were so many rides just waiting to be tried was next to impossible. As every minute passed, Joe pointed out, more and more people were spilling through the turnstiles like water gushing through the holes in a dam, and with more and more people the queues got longer and longer. It was time to move, the boys decided, and quickly.

The crowds were all flowing in the same direction, into the park and towards the rides. Joe and Mike darted amongst them, almost running, the hot sweet smell of cooking doughnuts wafting across from the nearby stands.

"We'll have some of those later," said Mike. Joe nodded and thought with irritation how that sounded like an order rather than a suggestion. He couldn't disagree though, he liked doughnuts as much as Mike did.

Everything about the park seemed designed to add cheer to a teenage boy's heart, the buttery sun reflecting off the glittering metallic balloons that danced above the information stands, the lovely looking girls at the information stands in their short skirts and low cut tops, everything except for the queues, even at this early hour they were getting long.

Joe and Mike joined the one for The Styx, a water ride. It would give them plenty of time to dry off if they did it early, Mike said. Joe wished that he could think of these sorts of things once in a while so that he could say them first and seem incisive and decisive before Mike did, even if it was just occasionally.

The queue wasn't too bad and within twenty minutes they were nearing the front of the queue. Mike was looking nervous and Joe had noticed that he'd grown progressively quieter the closer they'd got to the front of the line. He was even getting a little pale.

"You okay?" Joe asked.

Mike nodded.

"Yeah, just wish I'd gone to the bogs before we'd joined the queue. I'm bursting."

A few minutes later they were strapped inside a floating coffin that then began the long rattling haul up a steeply inclining track with water gushing down that splashed around the edges of the coffin. Mike hung on to the front while Joe peered around the side of his big curly head. Mike had taken his hat off when they had left their stuff in the locker and now his hair had sprung out in rock star fashion.

At the top of the incline the track levelled out and the coffin became horizontal again and then with barely a moment's warning it turned abruptly to the left and went into an inky tunnel.

All was silent save the lapping sounds of water and the nervous giggles echoing from the people behind. Then suddenly they were plummeting.

The boys gasped, stomachs left behind, air sucked out of them. They got it back just in time to yell in fear and delight before the coffin hit the end of the fall with a huge splash.

Joe heard Mike curse, he had insisted on sitting in front for the better view but now Joe was delighted to realise that Mike was actually just going to get wetter than him. It was so dark he wouldn't be able to see anything anyway.

The coffin levelled out and moved forward. It was utterly black, not the tiniest glimmer of light in the smothering shroud of darkness. This is what it must be like to be blind, thought Joe, or dead…

Suddenly a voice loomed through the silence, low, and agonized like the sound of a man locked in a dungeon with nothing but rats for company, the sound of a mind gone mad, clutching at the last strands of sanity.

"The River Styx is the river of the dead," intoned the voice. "All who die must cross the river, and all who live must die." There was a pause and then the voice started again only louder, higher pitched and madder. Joe heard Mike giggle nervously. "*ALL* must cross the river. And you…now it is *your* turn. Do you have a penny for the boat man? A silver penny? No? Oh dear…then you must go, my friend, to…HELLLLL"

"AAAAAAAAARGH!"

They were falling again, only further, steeper, faster.

Mike and Joe yelled in delight, full-blooded roars that echoed off the ceiling, then another drop, and they were further soaked.

The tunnel became silent, the cries and laughter dying away. The only sound was the quiet lapping of water. The coffin seemed hardly to be moving, just rocking slowly on the surface of the water, there wasn't even the tiniest glimmer of light.

Every sound was magnified, the sounds of the water rippling, of their rapid breathing, their hearts beating and the blood hissing in their ears, the quick nervous laughter of those in front and behind, every sound was maximised and made enormous.

Joe was acutely aware of his body, how it was squeezed into the small seat, how his arms were the only thing that could move freely. At the entrance there had been a sign, 'This ride is not suitable for those who suffer from claustrophobia'. Joe didn't think he had that or a fear of getting trapped, but still the darkness was beginning to feel oppressive like a blanket wrapped around his head, smothering him. His breathing began to rip from his lungs faster and shorter until he was not taking enough oxygen in and he was gripped by the ice cold hand of panic. A voice began running around the curved interior of his head, round and round, faster and faster. 'I have to get off I have to get out of here I must get out!' His mind was racing out of control, a rising tide of fear that was wrenching his mind into a craze of terror.

And then suddenly a thought appeared from nowhere, popped into his head, and he was calm again, a precious lung full of air expanding in his chest. He had realised that he couldn't be afraid if Mike wasn't. But what if Mike was? He was certainly a bit of a coward when it came to watching horror films. And if he wasn't, Joe knew how to make him afraid…

The coffin was still sliding slowly through the oblivion. Joe dipped his hand over the edge of the vessel's side and let it trail in the frigid water. Then, slowly, unable to see his own hand in front of his face he moved it gently forward until it brushed, cold, wet and clammy across the back of Mike's bare neck and, as he did so, Joe screamed horribly, right in Mike's ear.

The shriek that exploded from Mike filled the tunnel and echoed off the walls and was then joined by the screams of others further back who were either alarmed by the sound or thought it was all part of the experience.

"You bastard," Joe heard Mike mutter over the racket. "I'm going to get you for that." He heard Mike turning in his seat. "Dead leg coming up." Joe braced himself for the pain but Mike never got his punch in. The coffin lurched and then dropped fifteen feet.

Chapter 9

Revenge

Joe was already apologising as they got off the ride. Mike was soaked and his face had flared to a livid shade of crimson. Joe wasn't sure whether it was from anger or embarrassment, perhaps it was both. It didn't help matters that even as he was saying sorry, Joe was fighting back the laughter that was threatening to explode out of his mouth like an unstoppable mudslide that once free could not be contained.

Mike was so angry he couldn't even talk, he just shook his head and pushed Joe away, his mouth pursed in a pout of scarlet fury.

Joe realised that there was a wet mark on the front of Mike's jeans and that there was something about it that didn't look as though it had been caused by splashing. Joe couldn't say why exactly, it just didn't. Perhaps it was the way that the rest of the water splashes seemed to have been restricted to Mike's upper body, perhaps it was the way that the patch was on one side, the left, a round darkness that tapered off the further down his leg it went.

Coldness seized Joe and the laughter died inside of him. He remembered how Mike had needed the toilet in the queue. Then he remembered something that had happened years ago when they were in junior school. Joe had been the only one who hadn't screamed and laughed at the dark patch that had spread around Mike as they sat on the yellow carpet at story time.

Joe felt terrible, ashamed of what he had done to his friend. He felt the humiliation that must be filling Mike up like scalding liquid. Joe placed a cautious hand on Mike's shoulder but he shrugged it off angrily.

"I'm sorry, Mike. Really. It was really stupid. It wasn't funny. I'm a dick, Mike. I'm sorry."

Mike swivelled and glared at Joe, his pale blue eyes as cold as knives, the freckles on his nose twisted upward in a sneer. It was his shock at seeing the hatred in Mike's face that made Joe take a step back. He was glad there were lots of adults around because he was pretty sure that Mike would have punched him otherwise. The colour in Mike's eyes seemed to have faded to grey, glittering with metallic sharpness.

"Don't worry, Joe. You'll get yours," he said muttered. "You'll get it when you're least expecting it." He turned and stalked away.

Joe sighed and started to follow, letting Mike keep a small distance ahead. Perhaps he'll cool off, Joe thought to himself a little desperately.

He remembered when he'd taken the mickey out of a shirt Mike had bought. That had taken three days for him to get over, and now he'd made Mike piss himself. How much worse could it get? He plodded on after Mike's hunched and furious back.

Mike disappeared into the first toilets that he came to and Joe sat down on a bench outside to wait.

As he sat there in the sun Joe was torn between laughing at the memory of Mike's reaction in the tunnel - it was rare that Joe ever got one over on Mike – and regretting what he'd done. Mike could hold a grudge like no-one he knew. It could potentially ruin the whole two days if Joe couldn't find a way of making him realise that he was truly sorry.

When Mike eventually emerged from the toilet his clothes were still wet, but less so. He must have been standing under the hand drier, thought Joe. The patch on the front of his jeans was now mysteriously blended with the other areas of wetness, and Joe realised that he must have splashed water down his front to join the offending patch with the ones higher up.

Joe had done something similar once at school when he hadn't shaken properly and a long dribble of wee had slid down the inside of his thigh, staining his trousers. As he remembered this Joe realised that Mike had been merciless in his mockery once he realised what Joe had tried to do, going so far as to point it out to a couple of girls who had been standing nearby. He only stopped when Joe threatened him with a broken nose. The memory made Joe feel a whole lot less bad for what he had done to Mike.

Mike's expression, meanwhile, was still one of granite. He stood in front of Joe and spoke without making eye contact, tipping his head upwards and back slightly as though to avoid an unpleasant smell.

"I don't want to see you for the next hour. If I can stay away from you for that long then I might not smash your face in."

"Mike, I'm…"

Mike held up his hand, his palm in Joe's face.

"Shut up. I'm talking, you're listening. Be back here in an hour and you'd better hope I've calmed down or you won't see me again. And don't forget," Mike sneered, fixing his eyes on Joe. "I've got the key to the bike chain."

It was true, they'd locked their bikes together using Mike's D-lock. If he wanted, Mike could go and unlock his own bike and then lock Joe's up or hide it, then he could cycle back to Stonebridge leaving Joe stuck at Terror Hall. Joe would be forced to call his parents to get them to come and pick him up and then the cat would be out of the bag. He'd get no pocket money for months and he'd be grounded forever. He didn't think Mike would do it but if he *did* do it then Joe would make sure that Mike's mum found out as well, even if that was grassing. Joe he watched Mike walking away, his shoulders hunched and his hands in his pockets.

He leaned back on the bench and sighed. Opposite was a ride called To Hell and Back. Above the entrance the face of a devil, red and evil, looked down at Joe, meeting his eye.

Chapter 10

The Museum

Joe didn't really fancy queuing for rides on his own so he spent some time wandering around and thinking. He checked his phone but had no reception. He thought about switching it off altogether but something made him leave it on.

Thinking about his mum made him start thinking about Mike's family. It wasn't that they'd always been cruel or violent towards Mike, though they often had, the worst thing was that they'd just ignored him half the time. Now, of course, it was just Mike's mum but things were continuing just as they had before his dad had died. In fact, if anything they seemed to be getting worse. It was as though Mike's mum was taking her loss out on him.

Although he was usually skint Mike would sometimes have quite a lot of money. Whenever they had any, which was not often, his parents would chuck some at him to keep him quiet, but they never went anywhere as a family, and now that Mike's dad was dead even the sudden flushes of money had dried up. The only outings he ever really got to go on were those he was invited on with Joe's family.

Mike's brother, Stevie, was the only one who ever really showed Mike he was loved. It was amazing given their background that Mike and Stevie were such nice lads, even if they were daft and a bit light fingered.

Mike had told Joe that his Dad's side of the family used to have money but that they had drunk it all and the only inheritance his Dad had ever got from his own father was a love of the bottle. And then he had married Mike's mum, someone who shared his interests. Mike once said that he thought Stevie's dad, they only shared a mother, had been driven away by her boozing. Once again Joe found himself thinking how lucky he was to have such dull parents. Mike once said he was worried he might have inherited the family weakness for booze. Joe hadn't known what to say to that.

After wandering around for a while, wondering what to do next, Joe came across a sign for a museum. That sounded like something that he could do on his own, he thought. It would certainly beat wandering around alone Being by himself wasn't so bad, it was being *seen* to be alone that was the bad thing, as though you had no friends, as though you were diseased or had been rejected. Joe thought there weren't likely to be many people in the museum and those there would probably be old.

Joe consulted one of the maps that were dotted around the park. The museum was housed in the ruins of the old stately home that stood at the centre of Terror Park, the huge house where the people who used to own the land once lived.

Joe followed the signs along paths lined with grass, hedges and trees, moving through the crowds and the primary colours until he found himself walking towards a crossroads surrounded by wide lawns. The right hand turn led into a long line of spruces, obscuring its destination. He was intrigued as to where it went and on arriving at the crossroads he looked down the avenue and there, at the end of a long driveway, was the old stately home.

The driveway was as wide as a main road and was bordered on either side by the tall trees whose shade gave it a cold and dingy feel as though shunning the daylight and the sun. Joe walked its length until after twenty feet or so he arrived at a large gravel space bordered by a faded and overgrown lawn. Few visitors seemed to come to this part of the park. No one had bothered keeping it in very good order, but at one time, thought Joe, these lawns would have been impeccably manicured. This was the first thing the owners would have seen as they left their home and the first thing visitors would have seen as they approached the house and so it would have been kept in the best of possible order, designed to impress and please the eye. Despite the years and despite the neglect Joe could still see the faded glory.

The trees must have been late additions for now they served only to screen the magnificent old building from the rest of the park, thus depriving it of the incredible views that it must once have commanded over the acres of land under its dominion. From the gravel area where the visiting horse drawn coaches must have dropped their passengers a short flight of crumbling sandstone steps led up to the empty house, gutted by fire and never repaired. The building glared over its desecrated parkland like a huge empty skull. The windows gazed with disgust at the rollercoasters that loomed over the spruce trees, at the gaudy burger van at the end of the avenue, at the herds of people who had invaded from housing estates across Britain, grinning and gurning and dropping their litter with never a thought for the beauty that had been so painstakingly assembled. The house seemed infuriated, there was a feeling of hatred coming from the derelict building that fuzzed and crackled like static on a detuned television.

Joe stared uneasily up at the huge walls of the house. It was the one really interesting thing in the entire park, the one thing that people in a hundred, no, a thousand years would still be interested in, *if* it was still standing, which seemed unlikely as the people who ran Terror Hall appeared to have put almost no effort or money into looking after the building. It was almost as if they wanted it to look shabby and threatening to keep it in line with the gothic horror theme of the park.

Joe climbed the steps and saw an arrow to the left pointing to the entrance. He glanced up at the building again and saw, looking down from a third floor window, a man with a long pale face. He seemed to be wearing a hooded black cloak but it was hard to tell due to the gloominess of the room he was in, but what was certain was that the pallid face that floated in the darkness held an expression of disgust. The man's thin lips were twisted and his red rimmed eyes burned with hatred.

Joe felt himself go cold.

And then the face was gone, very suddenly, and it wasn't clear to Joe how the man had withdrawn his head so quickly or moved out of sight. It was as though he had vanished, vaporised before Joe's eyes. Joe frowned, he hadn't realised that some of the upper floors were open to the public. It certainly hadn't looked like it from where he had been standing further down the driveway. Everything looked so dark and abandoned.

I'll be able to get a good view from up there, he thought, as he followed the gravel pathway across the front of the house and then down a narrow alleyway at the side of the house.

The alleyway was narrow, the wall of the house on one side and a tall hedge of viciously spiked holly on the left. After fifteen feet or so Joe came to a peeling green wooden door and over the door was the sign 'Museum'. It hadn't even been written in scary writing, just normal font like you might find on a National Trust building.

It was quiet here. The sounds of the screams and the wheels and rails of the rides were muffled by the trees and the holly, the old crumbling stone of the house. It sounded, thought Joe, like a pillow was over his head or as if he was under water.

He tried the door. It was open, half of him had hoped that it might be locked, it was so quiet, so desolate. There was something deeply unsettling about the place. It even felt colder than anywhere else in the park. Joe shivered. The light of the sun was blocked out by the darkness of the towering trees and walls. That must be what it was, he thought to himself, that must be why he felt so uneasy, it was a sort of claustrophobia.

The door creaked under the pressure of his push and opened into a small dingy room with bare floorboards and an old wooden desk, behind which sat a shrivelled old man with wild hair on both the back and the sides of his head but absolutely none on the top of his greyish wrinkled scalp. The hair he had, curled out crazily over his hunched shoulders.

As Joe entered the man peered up from the book he was reading, his little grey eyes meeting Joe's over the top of his half-moon spectacles. The old man's face remained expressionless and his gaze remained steady.

From somewhere in the room came a deep steady ticking, a grandfather clock, Joe thought. He wanted to look around the room but felt unable to look away from the man's strange corkscrew eyes. Joe began to feel uncomfortable with the silence and the man's unwavering stare. He didn't feel scared, the old man was too small and puny to be physically threatening, but all the same, there was something odd about him and about the room itself. It smelled damp, worse than damp, like a drain or a mouldy old pond, but underneath that smell was another smell, something unpleasant, threatening even, but while it was a familiar odour Joe couldn't put his finger on what its source might be.

With a sudden scrape of his chair the old man leapt to his feet with such unexpected speed and agility that Joe took a step back.

"Hello young man," said the old man, a grin splitting his face to reveal, yellow uneven teeth and a single gold tooth. "And how might you be this fine day?"

"Very well, thank you."

"Good, good. Forgive me for my… impolite welcome. You see, I'm not used to visitors. You're the first this week, and when I do get them they tend to be older folk." He was rubbing his hands together and grinning. "Are you interested in history?"

"Yes." Joe hesitated. "It's my best subject."

"Gooood," said the man, rubbing his hands together.

It was true, Joe really did love history. He never read fiction, only history books. Why read something made up, he thought, when you could read something that had really happened. History was so full of amazing things that you could barely believe had really happened that it seemed a waste of time to read something that had been made up.

"Well," said the old man. "If you go through the door," he said pointing to the opening to his left, "and then up the stairs you'll find yourself in the exhibition." Joe looked to the door and then back at the man. He didn't want to let him out of his sight although he wasn't quite sure why. Something about him filled Joe with unease, almost dread.

As Joe looked back he saw something out of the corner of his eye, something on the desk, just to the right of the old man's book. It was something so unusual that he had to look directly at it to make sure that his eyes weren't deceiving him.

It was a skull, a human skull. A human skull that the old man was using as a paper weight for some yellowing dog eared sheaves of paper. The man followed his gaze and started to laugh.

"Oh, don't mind the Earl, he won't hurt you."

"Is it real?"

"Oh yes," replied the old man, leaning over and rapping the skull with his knuckles. It made a hollow sound. "He's real alright."

He picked up the skull and began throwing it from one hand to the other like a cricket bowler waiting to take his run up. Now it was the skull rather than the old man that Joe couldn't take his eyes off, its two empty sockets and its row of smiling yellow teeth. All of a sudden the man stopped juggling and thrust the skull under Joe's nose.

"May I introduce, Gerald, fifteenth Earl of Culwick, killed one hundred and eighty seven years ago out on the main road. He was nearly home, two miles to safety when a footpad got him. Know what a footpad is laddie?"

Joe shook his head.

"A highwayman, an old fashioned mugger. They used to hang about on dark lonely roads and steal from the unwary. Our Earl here was a foolish young man, he rode alone when all said he should not, and he rode at night when all said that he should not. Beware the darkness my young friend for there are things in the shadows that we miss until it is too late, things that do not appear during the day because daylight is their enemy. The painter may use light but there are many who practise their art using darkness. The footpad, young Sir, knocked him from his horse by way of a length of twine stretched from one tree to another, right across the road, and when the Earl was flat on his back, half dead from the blow and the fall, the villain emerged from his hiding place and cut the poor fellow's throat."

The old man pretended to look sad but Joe thought that he had told the tale with such relish that his look of melancholy had to be an act.

"Why isn't his head buried along with his body?"

The old man winked horribly.

"Who's to say his body is buried," and gestured to Joe to be on his way. "I'll be up there with you shortly, Sir, just as soon as I've finished this chapter."

Joe nodded and walked towards the door.

"Oh," called the old man, and Joe turned. "There was one more thing, about the Earl's body I mean. Despite it being the middle of summer and there not having been rain for a week and no river or pond within half a mile, his body when it was found was soaked to the skin, absolutely sodden. Now how could that be? And why?"

Joe shrugged.

"You'll find out I'll warrant," winked the man. Joe had to hide the shudder that rippled through him. There was something so creepy about the man. He turned and carried on towards the doorway.

As he stooped to pass under its low beam he realised what the odour was, he sometimes smelled it in Stonebridge when the wind was blowing in the wrong direction when he walked past the slaughterhouse.

It was the smell of blood, the smell of fresh blood.

Chapter 11

Stewing

Mike found himself next to a souvenir shop selling T-shirts and fluffy toys. He wasn't sure how he'd ended up there, he'd just been wandering aimlessly, staring at the floor, convinced that people could see the stain on his jeans and were laughing at him. The day was warm though and when he looked closely he saw that it had dried and left only the faintest tide mark.

In the toilet he'd given it a really good soaking as what had worried him even more than people seeing was the thought of smelling of wee like some tramp or old person. When he thought back to himself in front of the sink, all those boys and men casting curious glances at him, he could feel his cheeks burning with shame. That bastard! He was going to get Joe so badly. He'd never felt so ashamed and humiliated in his entire life. It was the worst feeling he'd ever had. Well, not the worst, but he didn't want to think about that.

Mike sat down on a bench opposite the shop and stared at the people were coming and going without actually seeing them. When a couple of pretty girls in short summer dresses walked past and smiled at him he met their eyes but his face remained blank. The girls giggled as they walked on but something about Mike's expression had unsettled them and they didn't look back.

What bothered Mike most was that Joe knew, that Joe had seen. He needed Joe to think he was smart and cool, not some panty wetter. Whatever happened between them now there would always be this incident lurking in the shadows. He knew Joe hadn't meant to do it and he knew Joe felt sorry for what he'd done and he'd say it didn't matter, but it *had* happened and it *did* matter. It would always be there, indelible, inerasable, and for that he couldn't help hating Joe. Joe had done something that could not be taken back, he had changed things forever.

But the question was, what should Mike do now? He knew what his dad would have said, 'punch his bloody lights out', and then he would have slumped back on the settee, staring at the television in an alcoholic haze. Perhaps not the best advice.

The last time he'd seen him Mike's dad had smelled of whisky. He'd smelled it as they'd passed in the hallway, just before his dad had left the house. It had only been ten in the morning. The police hadn't said anything but Mike knew. He was determined never to touch a drop of alcohol as long as he lived.

His mum was still drinking, if anything more than before, and she seemed to have found herself a new bloke already, some young bloke from the pub. Mike didn't like him one bit even though he seemed alright. He could have been the nicest bloke in the world but Mike would still have hated his guts.

Mike wished that he'd brought his cigarettes with him, it would have made him feel cool and mysterious instead of a lonely loser sat by himself on the bench. He was sure that he was attracting pitying stares from the passers-by.

Mike knew that he had to get Joe back somehow but he couldn't think how. What could he do?

Mike sighed and got up from the bench. His jeans were fine he was relieved to see. He went into the shop opposite and bought a can of Coke.

Outside in the sun he cracked it open, took a swig and began to wander again with no idea of where he was going.

After walking a dozen or so slow steps to nowhere a thought suddenly occurred that made him stop and visibly brighten, his shoulders went back and his head rose as his spine straightened. He knew exactly where it was that he had to go.

From somewhere, it was impossible to tell whether it was near or far away, there came a sudden deep and low rumble, a sound almost like a drawn out growl, a sound so deep, low and loud that it seemed to vibrate in the ground beneath Mike's feet. He stopped and like everyone else in the crowds around him he stared up into the cloudless sky, looking for the thunder clouds that weren't there.

Frowning slightly he walked on.

Chapter 12

The Upstairs Room

As Joe climbed the stairs he wished that he wasn't alone. There was something about the little man downstairs and his room that smelled of blood that filled Joe with a profound unease.

The spiral stairway wound upwards to the right. Joe remembered reading that was so that the defenders, those that were right handed anyway, could swing their swords at the attackers coming up the stairs who would not be able to use their own swords as well. Unless they were left handed of course. Joe thought that left handed knights must have really hated attacking castles as they must have known they were going to get shoved to the front when it came to trying to take the towers. Joe was left handed and the thought of this made him a bit more cheerful and relaxed, at least he wasn't a medieval knight. This wasn't a real castle though, it wasn't old enough, it was just built to look like one. No one could have done any fighting in these rooms, he thought, but he was wrong on that count, not that he would ever know.

The stairway opened onto a large room with a vast vaulted ceiling and tall windows that let in lots of light from both the front and rear of the building. Flags, pennants and tapestries, faded and frayed, hung from the bare stone walls. The bare and splintered floorboards creaked under his Nikes as he walked cautiously out into the centre of the room. Glass cabinets lined the walls and illustrations and framed pictures hung from nails on the bare stone of the walls.

Joe made his way over to the first cabinet. Inside were historical artefacts, swords, medals, pictures and other objects, all neatly numbered and labelled with an explanation, and at regular intervals were panels of text that told the history of the hall and its inhabitants. It was these that took Joe's immediate interest and so he began reading.

The land that makes up much of what is now Terror Hall was given to Sebastien de Tellier in 1089 as reward for his service to Guy de Bordes, a Norman knight fighting in the service of William the Conqueror. Sebastien de Tellier had assisted de Bordes in subduing local opposition to the new foreign overlords.

De Tellier had been particularly effective and particularly cruel in his destruction of any opposition to his master. He is said to have burned an entire village to the ground and put its occupants to the sword.

That village, which appears in the Doomsday book and lists at least 140 residents, was the village of Culwick and it stood roughly where you are standing now. After its destruction there were no residents left to object to the building of Sebastien de Tellier's fortified manor house that stood where Tellier Hall still stands today. Legend has it that the bodies of the slaughtered were cast into a huge pit that had been dug by the young men of the village before they too were butchered and thrown in after their loved ones.

Excavations made in the early twentieth century uncovered human bones that bore the marks of blows from sharp implements. It is thought that the vast majority of the villagers' bones still remain in the ground beneath Tellier Hall, making up its foundations.

As reward for his terrible services, Sebastien de Tellier was given an Earldom, newly created to honour his heinous feats, the Earl of Culwick.

Joe made the connection, Tellier Hall – Terror Hall, it was a terrible pun.

He read on, skipping over the less interesting passages until he came to the section that covered the 18th century.

The Eleventh Earl of Culwick, Robert de Tellier, improved the family fortunes considerably through some shrewd investments in sugar and tobacco plantations in the Caribbean and later in a company of slave traders who transported slaves from the west coast of Africa to the same Caribbean islands upon which he had his plantations.

The vast profits that this shameful trade realised allowed Robert de Tellier to purchase large tracts of land surrounding Tellier Hall, including some belonging to his destitute neighbour, the Earl of Troon.

It was on this land that the village of Hobsdor stood, a village numbering some eighty souls, and it was this village that fifty years later was to become the second that was removed from the face of the Earth by a member of the de Tellier family.

Intrigued, Joe scanned the pages of the display, walking along the cabinets until he came to the relevant passage. Fifty years later, he discovered, in 1776 Tellier Hall was in the hands of the Thirteenth Earl of Culwick, Charles de Tellier, the grandson of Robert de Tellier. He read on.

The Earl ordered the villagers from their homes, giving them a day's notice and no compensation, merely the news that their services were no longer required. Most of the villagers had lived there all their lives and had little or no experience of life outside the immediate vicinity. This was a time, one must remember, when many people knew not what lay beyond 'the next set of hills'.

One elderly man, who history records as being one Edgar Trundle, had been born in the house from which he was now being evicted and he saw fit to protest to the Earl and the men charged with his eviction, perhaps believing that his advanced years would see him spared ill-treatment. He was wrong.

The story goes that at a nod from the Earl one of his henchman battered the man to death with blows from the butt of a flintlock pistol. The man's corpse was left in the doorway of his cottage as his weeping wife was led away, carrying all that she could manage to bear.

As she left, however, she turned deliver a curse upon Charles de Tellier that would come back to haunt him and his ancestors for generations to come.

What Charles de Tellier did not know, and had he known it may not have stayed his hand, such was his ignorance, was that

Edgar Trundle's wife, whose name history does not record, was reputed to be the last in a long line of illustrious and powerful witches, women who had handed down their secret and arcane knowledge from mother to daughter ever since the Romans first brought Christianity to these shore and the pagan beliefs native to the British Isles were persecuted and driven underground.

There was a creak on the floorboards behind him. Joe tensed, realising that he could hear breathing and that it was immediately behind him. He turned, full of dread.

It was the old man, leaning forward, his face stretched in a gruesome leer.

Joe jerked backwards. How on Earth had the old man managed to move so silently? There was not a sound in the room to mask his approach. The floorboards were old and squeaked with every step. Even the sounds of the rides and the screams of the people riding them were muted in here. How had he made it across half the room so soundlessly?

"I'm sorry to alarm you, Sir," said the old man, his face thrust forward in a grimace of friendliness. His hands were behind his back and Joe had the uneasy sensation that he was hiding something. "Fascinating history isn't it?" the man went on. Joe nodded.

"Do carry on," said the old man, gesturing towards the display cabinets with one hand but taking care to keep the other concealed. "If you have any questions, don't hesitate to ask." He grinned a ghastly grin that revealed his yellow uneven teeth. "I shall be waiting over yonder," he said, pointing across to a high-backed wooden chair near the top of the stairs.

"Thank you," said Joe and watched him turn and walk across to the chair, the floorboards creaking as he went. As the man turned his back on Joe he moved the hand that had been hiding so that now it was in front, still concealing whatever was in it. Now Joe was certain he was holding something, but what could it be? What could it be that needed to be hidden?

Joe turned back to the cabinets, deeply uneasy at having the man at his back, but still he read on.

Charles de Tellier had employed a famous architect, Erasmus McIndoe, to landscape the fields and valleys that had been acquired by his grandfather. It was de Tellier's ambition to create a stately home with scenic landscapes that were unequalled in England, and in this he can have been said to have succeeded.

The main feature of McCindoe's plan for the estate that was laid out before Charles de Tellier was for a lake that would cover at least two square miles in its totality. The lake was to be created by damning the river that flowed through Hobsdor. The fact that Hobsdor would be lost to the world, drowned under hundreds of thousands of gallons of water, was of little consequence to either McCindoe or de Tellier, and so the evictions and the flooding took place, creating, it is generally agreed, a lake of great beauty and peaceful appearance.

It is only when one discovers what lies beneath that one's sense of tranquillity is disturbed and the truth of the human suffering that was created in order that the lake be brought into being is realised.

Joe looked across at the old man. He was back in his chair and deeply engrossed in a book that he held in his lap and did not seem to notice Joe looking at him. Joe turned back and continued reading.

The waters, as they rose, covered the village in its entirety, but it is said that in hot summers, when the rainfall is poor and the water levels drop, that one can still see the top of the Hobsdor church, its spire emerging from the gloomy waters. Some even say that its bells can be heard at night, chiming bleakly beneath the windswept surface of the water.

Though no such sighting have been made for many years, divers wearing the latest breathing apparatus have recently discovered a number of houses and the remains of a church, although the church tower itself appears to have collapsed.

This story is not without tragedy as on two occasions divers have found themselves in difficulties whilst exploring the subaquatic ghost town, and two have lost their lives. One of these men's bodies has never been recovered.

It has been proposed on a number of occasions that explosive charges should be dropped from a boat positioned above the submerged village in order to destroy any remaining buildings and thus remove the temptation for any other divers to risk their lives in foolish exploratory expeditions.

The lake was also meant to provide a water-born distraction for the Earl, his family and his guests, but strange currents, unseen from above, swirl about the depths of the lake and make boating and swimming a hazardous and occasionally fatal proposition.

This was discovered shortly after the flooding of the lake was completed when a boat containing the Earl's youngest son, Ivor, and his nurse, was capsized and the two unfortunates were sucked down into the watery depths of the unnatural lake, their bodies never to be recovered.

Some have said that these two were the first victims of the curse.

And what was the curse that the woman, Mrs Trundle, is said to have shouted to Charles de Tellier? It is, of course, impossible to verify what her actual words were, but contemporary accounts describe her screaming through her tears that as water would destroy Hobsdor so water would destroy the de Tellier family, that their very doom would rise from the depths to steal their luck and their loved ones, and so it came to be.

A heavy hand fell on Joe's shoulder. He stifled a scream and wriggled out from under the claw-like grip that had seized him.

"Interesting, eh?" smiled the man, unconcerned by Joe's reaction to his touch.

Joe nodded, trying to compose himself.

"I have to be going," he stuttered, pointing at his watch. "I'm supposed to be meeting my mate. I should have been there five minutes ago."

Looking down at his watch he realised that this was, in fact, true. Where had the time gone? Mike would go mad. Madder. Joe bolted past the man and ran for the stairs.

"Stop right there, young man," the old man ordered, and there was something in his voice that made Joe stop, a note of command that had to be obeyed. He turned to see the old man walking slowly towards him, his left hand again concealed behind his back.

"I have a gift for you," the old man said through a sickly grin.

Joe wanted to run but his legs would not move. The old man was getting closer, his eyes never leaving Joe's. When he was three feet away he stopped and whipped his hand out from behind his back, shoving what he was holding under Joe's nose.

"Something to read in the queues, young man."

It was a couple of booklets, simple A5 stapled booklets that looked as though they were home made, printed from a PC and then put together by hand. Joe took them cautiously.

"I wouldn't let you have these unless I felt sure that you'd appreciate them, and there are few young folk who read the displays as you have done," he leered.

"Thank you," said Joe, feeling strangely flattered by the man's words. He looked down at the pamphlets. *The Curse of the de Tellier Family* read one, *A Brief History of 'Terror Hall' and the de Tellier Estate* read the other. Joe rolled them up together into a tube and slid them into the back pocket of his jeans.

"I'll read it soon. Thanks. Thanks a lot," he said.

Although he was desperate to get away from him Joe actually felt rather proud that the old fellow should have given him the pamphlets. He decided to ask a question before he left, his fear now diminished. Later he would wonder if perhaps the old man had somehow hypnotised him.

"What's on the floors above?" Joe asked, thinking of the long pale face he had seen from outside, the one peering down from the upper window.

"Upper floors?" said the old man raising his eyebrows. "This is the upper floor. The other two are completely derelict, without floorboards even. Without beams. They've been that way since the great fire of 1936. You'll read about that in the pamphlets I gave you."

But that couldn't be, thought Joe, that couldn't possibly be, he had seen a face, he had definitely seen the face of a man up there. A shiver ran through him and something about the way the old man was looking at him, or rather leering at him, made him realise it was time to leave, and fast.

"Enjoy your stay," called the man.

It wasn't until Joe was out of the building and running towards the spot outside the toilets where he was supposed to meet Mike that he realised that what the old man had said was rather strange.

Enjoy your day, perhaps, but enjoy your *stay*.

Chapter 13

Meeting with Mike

By the time he arrived back at the toilets Joe was slightly out of breath from the run. He sat down on the bench where he was supposed to meet Mike and checked his watch. He was alarmed to see that he was almost ten minutes late.

Leaning forwards, trying to slow his breathing, Joe scanned the passing crowds, searching for Mike. At least Mike wouldn't be able to moan at him for being late. Or perhaps Mike had already turned up, perhaps he had waited five minutes and then, furious at Joe for not being on time, he had carried out his threat and gone home.

Or perhaps he was never going to come back in the first place, perhaps he had just gone straight to the coach park, taken his bike and headed home, sending Joe off on a wild goose chase in order to give himself an hour's head start, leaving Joe stranded.

Joe began to feel himself sweating. He pulled his phone out of his pocket, wondering if he should call his mum and come clean about his deception. She could come and get him and put an end to this sorry mess. He was getting ahead of himself, blowing things out of all proportion, looking for the worst possible outcome, he told himself. That was one of Joe's problems, pessimism. He always had to remind himself that things might actually turn out alright. He had sometimes wondered why he was like that, nothing bad had ever really happened to give him reason to be so negative.

Joe sighed and looked at his phone to see if he had missed any calls – perhaps Mike had tried to call while he was in the museum – but saw that he still wasn't getting any signal. The whole park seemed to be a dead zone. They were a long way from any big towns, perhaps that was why. But then he'd got a signal at the abandoned railway station and that had been just outside the gates of Terror Hall. Surely the mobile phone companies would want to get reception in a huge tourist attraction.

And then, suddenly, as if from nowhere, something spoke inside Joe's head, some voice of intuition, some sixth sense, and he realised that Mike hadn't gone anywhere, that Mike had been here on time and had been here all along, and that right at that minute he was hiding somewhere, watching him. Joe stood up and looked around. He realised that if Mike was hiding then he didn't want to be discovered, and that if he was found it would only make him angrier. Once he had spotted him he could pretend that he hadn't, and could then sit down again and wait for Mike to come over in his own good time.

Joe spotted him almost immediately, lurking in the shade of an enormous purple umbrella attached to an ice-cream trolley. The trolley was manned by an overweight teenager in a pastel uniform who was selling huge cones of pink and yellow ice-cream which were impaled with chocolate flakes and slathered on top with whipped cream. Mike was there, hiding behind the queue, his eyes fixed on Joe.

Joe allowed his eyes to pass over the spot where Mike was as though he hadn't seen him, as though his eyes were focussed at a different distance. One thing that Joe had that was better than Mike was his eyesight. Joe had fighter pilot's eyes, 20/20 vision, whereas Mike needed to wear glasses but refused to. He said that he hated the feel of them on his nose and his ears, but Joe knew that it was really because Mike was vain. Mike had almost certainly failed to notice Joe's eyes locking onto his for that split second before they'd moved on, and he would certainly not have seen the flare of triumph and recognition that blazed there for the briefest of moments. Joe felt that whatever might now come, he had got one over on Mike simply by spotting him, and now he knew what game it was that Mike was playing.

Joe sat back down again. He realised that what Mike wanted was to make Joe feel sorry for what he had done to him. If Joe could convince him that he *did* feel sorry then maybe Mike could let it go and they could get on with having fun, with having their adventure. Joe took a deep breath, leaned forward and put his head in his hands. He considered heaving his shoulders to make it look as though he was crying but realised that would be overdoing it. Mike would almost certainly think that he was taking the piss.

It worked, after five minutes Joe heard footsteps approaching and then Mike's voice.

"You're late."

Joe looked up. He noticed that Mike's trousers had dried off in the sun, but that there was still a small tide mark on his jeans where he had had his accident. He looked away, he didn't want Mike to catch him looking at the source of his shame and the source of their argument.

"Not as late as you. How could you know I was late if you've only just got here?"

Mike was silent, Joe had called his bluff and for a moment he wished he hadn't. He needed to hand Mike this little victory if things were to be smoothed over. Joe stood, slouching to allow Mike to be slightly taller, and offered his hand for Mike to shake.

"Mates? I'm sorry Mike. It was stupid."

"Yeah it was," Mike grunted, taking Joe's hand and giving it a half-hearted shake. "Just never tell anyone, okay?" he said rubbing his nose and failing to make eye-contact.

"Yeah, obviously," Joe grunted back. "Come on," he went on in a dismissive tone as though he had already forgotten about Mike's accident and would never remember it again. "I want to go on Silver Bullet."

He gave Mike a grin and, after a moment where it felt to Joe that their whole trip hung in the balance, Mike grinned back.

What neither of them realised, as they walked away, was that someone was watching them, and this time the spy didn't need to gaze into an ancient wooden bowl to do so, he was right there with them.

They got to Silver Bullet and joined the queue that snaked down the railed path. The red electronic words on the digital signs informed them at regular intervals that they would be waiting for at least thirty five minutes. They were the last in line, a very long line that took a tiny shuffle forward every thirty seconds or so. Nevertheless everyone in the queue seemed content to wait, enjoying the sunshine and the company of their friends. Everyone except Mike.

"What a load of crap," he grumbled.

"Nah," replied Joe. "It'll go really fast."

Behind them an enormously fat couple in brightly coloured shorts and T-shirts joined the queue. At least now they weren't last, thought Joe. The couple must have been in their early forties. The man had a moustache and the woman constantly dabbed a handkerchief to her sweating face. They seemed excited and held hands.

Joe leaned in to Mike's ear and whispered.

"Think they'll fit into the cars?"

Mike glanced back and on seeing the couple his face cracked into a cruel grin which the woman saw. She smiled back awkwardly although Joe was pretty sure he could see it in her eyes that she knew Mike's smile was mocking.

He took Mike's shoulder, a hollow feeling in his stomach swelling with shame, turning him to face forwards again.

The fat couple's conversation had suddenly dropped to almost a whisper whereas before it had been loud and punctuated with laughter. Joe hardened his heart and reminded himself that something had to be done to get Mike out of his bad state of mind and that it was just too bad if the people behind had to suffer.

"It's ridiculous," Mike grumbled. "Imagine if you came a long way, London say. You'd travel for, what, three hours here, and then another three hours back which would give you, say, four hours here. Now, if you have to queue for half an hour for each ride, and then spend time on the rides, walking between them, having lunch, going to the toilet and all that, you'd only get to go on about six rides. And when you think, those rides are over in about two minutes tops, that would mean that in four hours you'd only spend around twelve minutes on the rides. Imagine that! Six hours of travelling, and all for twelve minutes on the rides!"

Joe could see that Mike was entrenched in one of his negative states. He must have been thinking about the logistics of travel and queuing for quite some time to have been able to come out with such a spiel.

Joe realised he was going to have to snap Mike out of this current state of mind, a state of mind where everything became a cause to moan. Mike could get like this, he was usually so happy and bubbly, but then something could knock the sunshine out of him and all would be gloom and doom. Joe knew that he could bring him out of it, but he would have to get on and do it quickly, before it was too late.

"Yeah," he said, agreeing with Mike. "It's dumb when you think about it. Good job we've got two whole days, and all for the price of one! We can take our time."

Mike nodded.

"'Spose so."

"Check out the map I got from the information stand," Joe added, pulling the colourful sheet of glossy paper from his back pocket. He had picked it up on his way to the museum. It was rolled up inside the leaflets the old man had given him.

"Look," Joe said, showing Mike the map. "We can plan where we want to go."

As the two boys shuffled along the slowly moving queue they studied the map. Joe said that he wanted to go on The Pit and the Pendulum, a huge swing that rocked backwards and forwards until eventually it went all the way around, pausing at the top to leave everyone on board suspended upside down. Mike wanted to go on Frankenstein's Lab, a tower in which the rider shot up and down surrounded by flashes of lightning and screaming monster faces. They both wanted to go on The Vampire, a rollercoaster that was supposed to be the fastest in Europe, and both were agreed that The Castle of Udolpho, which was little more than a glorified ghost train, looked pretty lame.

Silver Bullet was a rollercoaster based on the theme of werewolves. It was the newest ride at Terror Park, the one that had been featured on all the adverts and was the one that they had talked most about going on. They talked about the pictures they had seen on the internet and on TV and about all the things they had heard and read about it. Mike said that you actually travelled as fast as a bullet from a gun when you accelerated from the starting point. Joe thought that this was a bit unlikely but kept quiet. Surely it would cause a sonic boom if that was the case, he thought to himself, and he hadn't heard any large bangs since they'd arrived. Both Mike and Joe agreed that Silver Bullet was said to have the biggest drop of any rollercoaster in the world and then a triple loop at the bottom of that drop. If you had any heart problems then this ride would surely finish you off, said Mike, revelling in the fact that they were both young and could never be affected by such things. They were young, they were invincible.

Nothing could touch *them*.

The queuing was made even less boring by the presence of three saucy looking girls, two brunettes and a slightly dumpy blonde, a giggling trio of glittering eyes, laughing mouths, and cheap make up. They joined the line behind the stout couple who had joined after Mike and Joe.

Although neither Joe and Mike or the girls said a single word to each other they spent thirty minutes catching each other's eyes and then smiling and sniggering and whispering to their respective friends. The couple sandwiched between them didn't know whether to be irritated or amused by the interplay. They seemed glad that they weren't the focus of any attention although Joe suspected that the woman was anxious in case any of the laughter was at her expense. Joe for his part was happy to have the couple there as a buffer against the girls, if he had been made to speak to one of them he was sure that his face would have flushed as red as ketchup and his words would have tumbled out in a messy stutter of nonsense. Mike would have been alright, he'd have been calm and made them laugh while Joe stood awkwardly behind him trying to make his smile seem natural. The more that he tried to make it look natural the more certain it would be that it looked forced and phoney, the longer that he held the bogus expression the more that it would feel painful and twisted. Although his mouth might be up at the corners and his teeth might be showing whitely in a grin his eyes would betray him, uptight and scared. He grin would become more of a grimace, a terrifying leer that would be guaranteed to send any female running horrified from his presence.

Joe wondered if he would ever get himself a girlfriend.

Finally, after what seemed like an age, they arrived at the head of the queue and waited for the silver cars to roll into the platform. The wheels rumbled ominously on the rails as it appeared. The people on board were flushed and grinning. The seat bars rose and they clambered out of the cars, jabbering excitedly to one another. Watching these people and seeing how thrilled they were made the anticipation all the greater.

The boys waited for the last of the riders to get out of the cars and for the gates in front of them to open and then they climbed aboard.

The girls didn't make it on and stood at the head of the queue waiting for the next ride and watching the boys. Joe could feel their eyes watching him and everything he did, every move he made, however little seemed forced and unnatural. He couldn't relax despite telling himself that it would be Mike they would be watching, not him.

As the safety harness was clamped down over his shoulders, Joe could feel his heart rate increasing and his breathing becoming shallower. He always got a little bit nervous just before a ride, he didn't know why, nothing ever went wrong did it? And he always enjoyed the rides, so what was there to be afraid of? Perhaps it was that little doubt that played in the back of his mind, the possibility that something hadn't been checked, that a screw was loose, and that, while travelling at top speed the car would come free of the tracks and then…

"Look." Mike nudged him and nodded across to the entrance gate. The girls were all laughing and waving at Joe and Mike. Now that they were separated by the gate and there was no chance of a conversation the girls were emboldened. Joe tried to look nonchalant and cool and waved back as well as he could with his arm restrained by the harness. He felt stupid and felt fairly certain that they were actually waving at someone else, even though he knew they weren't. Joe was used to taking a doubtful approach to life and especially to girls.

Around them rang the sound of wolves howling. 'The blonde haired one's looking at me!' was his last pleasantly surprised thought before there was a loud bang and his body was hurtled through the air, faster and faster until he thought he might pass out.

Chapter 14

Silver Bullet

Joe often found himself getting ideas and thinking thoughts in the most unusual and unlikely of places and so it occurred to him as the Silver Bullet hurtled around the triple loop, screams of fear and delight ringing in his ears, that while Mike seemed to have come back around to the idea of the two of them being friends, he could actually be bluffing. Mike had threatened to get even with Joe and he usually meant what he said. He had once told Joe that a threat was nothing unless you were prepared to carry it out. If you didn't, all other threats you made would be empty and meaningless and you'd end up as a laughing stock. Joe was pretty sure that this had come from Mike's dad. Still, he had seen Mike carry out a threat once on a boy from the year above.

Mike's ears stuck out a bit, that was another of the reasons, Joe suspected, that Mike wore his hair long. For several days running whenever the older boy had passed Mike in the corridor he had flicked his ears and then walked away, laughing with his mates. On the last occasion Mike grabbed the boy's wrist before he had a chance to flick him and then, staring up at the older boy with blazing blue eyes, had told him in a calm and quiet voice that if he ever flicked his ears again he'd spread his nose across his face. The boy had walked off laughing nervously and trying to make a joke out of it, but Joe had seen that the boy's friends were mocking him and that the boy was annoyed by this, his face had been red and his smile forced and Joe had known that it wouldn't be the end of the matter.

Sure enough, the following day the boy had come up behind Mike and with two hands had flicked both ears as hard as he could, yelling triumphantly as he did so. Joe waited for the explosion but it didn't come, Mike had done nothing, just turned and stared at the boy with a blank expression that Joe knew meant trouble. The boy had crowed at Mike, thinking himself redeemed for the previous day's embarrassment, and then shouted to Mike as he walked away that he was all mouth and no trousers. Mike had still done nothing, just stared after the boy with his horrible bloodless gaze. It was like the stare of a killer, Joe had thought.

Later that day when the school bell had gone, Mike had ambushed the boy at the gates, swinging his school bag into the boy's face and spreading his nose across his cheeks in a squeltering crunch of blood and cartilage. He had then leapt on top of the boy as he lay gasping on the floor, his nose bubbling, and delivered two more smacks to his face before the boy's friends had been able to pull him off.

Mike got three days suspension for that but he said it was worth it. The boy certainly never flicked his ears again. His nose never looked the same either. Joe would never have done such a thing and he was glad he was that way. The sounds of Mike's fists landing in the older boy's face had made him feel sick.

Another thing worrying Joe was that Mike had said that he would get Joe when he was least expecting it, and if that was the case then what better way to make Joe unsuspecting than for Mike to pretend that he had forgiven him and that everything was okay. It wasn't a very comforting thought and Joe was feeling distinctly uncomfortable as its possibilities burrowed deeper into his mind.

Silver Bullet lived up to Mike and Joe's expectations. They got off wobbly with adrenalin and excitement, both of them babbling about the ride. It was a sharp contrast to how they'd felt after they left the water ride.

At the photo hut by the exit Mike spotted their picture on the TV screens, wide eyed and screaming. Mike had somehow known where the camera was and had made one of his fists into a pair of V's. The boys both laughed as they looked at the picture on the screen but didn't have enough money to buy a copy.

As they walked away to find another distraction a figure who had been standing motionlessly in the shade of a willow tree broke away from its darkness and with squinted eyes walked up to the photo hut. He pointed out Joe and Mike's picture to the young woman behind the counter who then went to print a copy off. She handed it to him and he thanked her, walking away without paying. The woman behind the counter moved on to the next customer, unconcerned that the man had failed to hand over any money.

After ten feet or so the old man from the museum stopped and studied the picture again. He had greased his long hair and combed it back so that it clung glistening to his skull. A slight smile twisted the corners of the man's mouth giving his face the look of a jack o' lantern. There was something in the lines on his forehead and the way he narrowed his eyes that spoke of determination.

Meanwhile, Mike and Joe and were heading for the ornamental gardens. Mike had decided they had something important to do and that the rides would have to wait. He was talking excitedly about it to Joe.

"I found a really good place for tonight, while you were doing…whatever it was that you were doing."

"I went to the museum. It was really…"

"Yeah," he said giving Joe a dismissive wave of the hand. "I'm not that interested to be honest."

Mike carried on talking but Joe found his thoughts slipping back into his suspicions around Mike's intentions. They walked on, the intensity of Joe's thoughts cutting out his surroundings so that he barely registered what he was walking past, let alone what it was that Mike was blathering about.

When Joe started thinking then nothing could get through the iron-cladding of his contemplation. Well, almost nothing.

He became aware that Mike was looking directly at him and repeating something. Joe hadn't heard a word that Mike had said for the past five minutes. He'd been so engrossed in his thoughts that he hadn't even noticed where they'd been going and looking up he realised that they had walked away from the main body of the park and were about to enter the ornamental gardens.

Mike punched him on the arm.

"Hello, hello? Earth to Joseph! Are you receiving? Is there anybody at home? Duhhhh." He rapped his knuckles on Joe's forehead.

"Gerrof." Joe slapped Mike's hand aside.

"Where were you? Did you listen to *anything* I just said?"

"Shut up. Course I did. I was just thinking about my mum, hoping she hasn't tried calling again," Joe lied. "There's no reception."

Mike slapped his palm to his forehead.

"Stop worrying about that, and get with what's going on here and now. You're about to walk into the jungle, the wilderness." He paused, attempting to let the importance of what he was saying sink in and then spoke slow and loud, as though to a stupid person. "The place where we are going to spend the night."

Joe peered down the path that led darkly off under the trees before bending out of sight after twenty yards or so.

With a crunch of gravel under his feet Mike started walking off down the path.

"Come on, numb nuts," he called back over his shoulder at Joe. "We haven't got all day. There are rides to go on. Follow me."

Joe took a deep breath and set off down the path after Mike. He had a bad feeling.

He was right to.

Chapter 15

The Hide

"What do you think?" asked Mike with an expectant grin. They were standing inside a large bush, or at least, that's what it looked like to Joe. It was an Asian flowering plant that grew upwards and outwards, its inside parts dying as a new layer of branches and roots took hold on the outside. As the inside parts decomposed they left an empty space of barren ground and it was in this that Mike and Joe were standing.

The space in the centre was considerable, easily big enough for two teenage boys to lie at full length with plenty of room to store their bags at their sides. The ring of foliage was at least six feet high and several feet deep so that no one passing would have any idea that people might be within the bush. It was also light as there was no ceiling to the plant, and only a few overarching trees nearby. In fact the whole place was quite agreeable, the sweet spicy scents of the plant's huge bell shaped white flowers making it a fragrant hiding place.

Joe nodded.

"Great," he said. "Brilliant."

Mike was beaming.

"Isn't it! Quite a place I reckon. Only took me half an hour to find it. No one will be able to see us in here and the flowers will probably put any dogs off our scent. I've got that spray that Stevie gave me as well."

"Yeah, I don't think we'll do any better than this," agreed Joe.

The other benefit of the plant was that on one side it was set off the nearest path by at least eight feet at the top of a low rise, and on the other it backed onto an impenetrable tangle of foliage that went on for as far as either boy could see.

However, on that far side, opposite where their hole led in, there was another hole, probably made by a fox or a badger. It didn't seem very likely that anyone, any intruders or pursuers, would be coming through from that direction as it was only just about big enough for boys to fit through. In a jam, Joe thought, it would serve as an emergency exit.

"I'd thought that we'd have to take it in turns to stay awake and keep watch," said Mike. "But this is so, what's the word, secluded, that I don't think we need to bother."

At that moment an electronic jangle filled the leafy space. It was Joe's phone. The two boys looked at each other.

"I thought you said there was no signal," said Mike.

"There wasn't," frowned Joe, pulling the phone from his jeans. He glanced down at the display. It wasn't his mum's number and he didn't recognise the number. He clicked the call answer button. There was silence.

"Hello?" said Joe.

Silence. But it wasn't complete, it was a silence that meant that someone was on the other end of the line, a hiss, a buzz, a sensation of someone. Someone or something.

"Hello?" he repeated.

From down the line came a laugh, a watery gurgle, a drain choked with bilious liquids, bubbling and belching with foul smelling gasses.

"Who is it?" Joe snapped. His voice was a little louder than he had intended.

Mike looked up when he heard the tone in Joe's voice.

"Who is it?" Joe repeated, slightly calmer, getting a grip on himself.

From the other end came another grotesque chuckle, a laugh of bad intention, a laugh of cruelty.

"No one for you, sonny boy," came a gurgling voice, low, thick and slick, as though from somewhere nearby, but at the same time, distant.

"What do you want?" Joe hissed.

"Something," bubbled the voice. "Just my little something. It's time, you see."

"What are you talking about, you freak," Joe shouted.

"Oh, you know," laughed the voice. "Nothing. Just…a, you know, wrong number." Again there was the laugh, a laugh only ever heard in dreams, bad dreams. And then there was nothing. Whoever it was had rung off. Joe snapped his phone shut.

"What's wrong," asked Mike.

"What are you on about?" Joe replied, trying to sound nonchalant.

"Oh nothing, just that you were yelling down the phone and you've gone white as a sheet," said Mike. "Was that your mum?"

"Course it wasn't," Joe spat, his face red.

"So…who was it?"

"Dunno, a weirdo. Wrong number." Joe hoped in some corner of his heart that this was true but he knew that it wasn't. He didn't know why, there was just something that told him, some sixth sense. "Let's get back to the rides," Joe muttered, and with that he was on his knees and wriggling out through the tunnel.

Before Mike had a chance to follow him, Joe was clear of the bush and walking down the slope and back to the path.

Mike had stared after him for a moment as he disappeared into the tunnel and then after a second or so, as though slapped from a waking dream, he lurched into life and followed.

Neither of the boys had seen the two yellow eyes that had been watching them from deep in the foliage. Both of the eyes were at least a foot across and they burned with a hunger and a madness that had sat for centuries, congealing and growing more toxic.

As Mike followed Joe out of the bush and made his way down to the path, the eyes, very slowly, blinked.

Chapter 16

Blood Burger

The boys made their way through the bustling crowd. Mike seemed so excited by their den that all thoughts of revenge seemed to have passed from his mind as had any disquiet at Joe's reaction to the telephone call.

That was typical of Mike, thought Joe, able to push bad thoughts to the back of his mind. The problem was that they tended to fester there. Joe hoped Mike's thoughts of revenge had truly disappeared and weren't just mouldering and getting worse. As for the phone call, Joe decided that he would try to push that to the back of his own mind. It was better to let it fester, he decided, and deal with it later than to let it ruin the day.

They were both getting hungry and decided to get some food before going on the next ride. Before long they spotted a glass fronted building in the style of an American diner, its frame and roof painted gothic red and black. A huge neon sign declared its name, Blood Burger, one of Terror Hall's own fast food restaurants that were scattered around the park.

They got their food from the counter and found a free table. Everything had a themed name. Mike had a Bloody Burger with Ghoulash dressing while Joe had a Torture Rack of Prisoner's Ribs, although they were actually just pork ribs in sweet and sour sauce. The chips were called Fried Alive Fries.

As they got stuck into their lunch Joe pulled the map of the park from his back pocket and laid it out on the table in front of them. It was brightly coloured and bold lines showed the paths while different colour shadings showed different zones. Little pictures accompanied each ride's name to give some idea of what they might be like. A snaking line of jagged grey represented the narrow gauge railway that transported people around the park.

Right in the centre of the page, and thus the park, Joe noticed Tellier Hall. Just off to the left of that was a large area that represented the gardens where they would be bunking down for the night, and beyond that, taking up an even larger space, was a blue expanse that represented Hobsdor Lake.

It suddenly occurred to Joe that perhaps the voice on his phone could have been the museum man playing some sort of sick joke, but then he dismissed it almost as soon as he had thought of it. The voice on the phone was different, unearthly somehow, and besides, how could the old man have got his number? And on top of that, why on earth would he want to waste his time making such pathetically weird calls? Unless he was a pathetic weirdo.

Or a complete madman.

Joe shook the thought from his mind.

"We're here right?" said Mike pointing at a Blood Burger sign on the map. "What's the 'ice house'?" he asked, pointing to a yellow dot on the map just to the left of where they were.

"It's a cave dug out and lined with turf. It meant that the rich people in Tellier Hall were able to get ice for their drinks even in the summer. They'd get some ice from the lake in winter to get it started and then once it was cold inside they could make ice at any time of the year. It's basically a non-electric fridge."

"How come you know so much?" exclaimed Mike.

"I've been looking at this," Joe replied, holding up the copy of *A Brief History of 'Terror Hall' and the de Tellier Estate* that the old man had given him. "I read some of it while we were in the queue for Silver Bullet, and when I was waiting for you outside the toilets."

"Oh," replied Mike turning away. He wasn't very interested in history but Joe told him anyway, he told him about the drowned village, about how the narrow gauge railway that ran about the estate had been built by one of the de Tellier family who had become interested in the new technology emerging during the nineteenth century. He had used it to bring in coal to fuel the house and to ferry his guest around his estate to impress them with its size and majesty. The park now used the railway to allow visitors to get around the grounds from ride to ride.

Joe told Mike about the de Tellier family curse and at that Mike's ears pricked up. He was always fascinated by tales of the supernatural and anything remotely macabre.

Joe produced the leaflet that the old man had given him, *The Curse of the de Tellier Family*. Joe hadn't had a chance to read any of it yet but he told Mike everything he knew so far from what he had read in the museum and told Mike that there was more in the leaflet.

"Read it to me," said Mike. He wasn't much of a reader himself but he didn't mind listening.

"Let's decide what we're going to go on first," said Joe, "and then I can read it to you while we're in the queue."

"Okay. What then?"

"Only one choice isn't there?"

"Vampire?"

"Obviously!"

They both laughed. Perhaps he really has forgotten about his threat, thought Joe as they headed for the door.

Chapter 17

The Curse of the de Tellier Family

Joe read Mike all the stuff about the village being flooded, the old man's death and his wife's curse on the de Tellier family, and then the death of Ivor, the youngest son of the Earl, and his nurse, that followed, although there was one detail that he hadn't heard before.

The village that had been flooded to make the lake had been named Hobsdor – he knew that already - and the writer of the pamphlet thought that the name probably came from the two words 'Hobb's' and 'door'. 'Hobb' he went on to say was an old word for imp, goblin, or devil. Perhaps Hobsdor was the Devil's door, from Hell up to Earth, the writer suggested. It would, he said, explain some of the evil events that came about as a result of the village being flooded. And was it merely a coincidence that a hundred years after the flooding, Albert, seventeenth

Earl of Culwick, reputedly sold his soul to the devil in an attempt to escape the clutches of the curse that afflicted his family?

That was interesting, thought Joe, perhaps there would be more on that later on. He continued to read and now it was even more interesting for him as he had got past the things he had read about in the museum. Mike listened in silence.

So engrossed were the two boys that on a couple of occasions the people behind them in the queue had to tell them to move forward as the line had moved on.

The ill-fortune of the de Tellier family all seemed to be connected to water; another de Tellier child drowned in four inches of bath water, five slave ships that represented a huge investment of the family money sank with all hands and all of the unfortunate slaves.

Philip, Fourteenth Earl of Culwick, whose money had been thus tied became convinced that the souls of the sailors and slaves were haunting him to avenge their deaths. He committed suicide by leaping from the cliffs at Dover and into the foaming waters of the sea that crashed on the rocks below.

A strange detail of the story is that on the night before each death or disaster a strange noise is said to be heard coming from Hobsdor Lake.

The writer went on to describe the noise carefully and at length, drawing on the descriptions of those who had heard it.

...a massive sound, a low ominous vibration that filled the air and trembled the glass in the windows of Tellier Hall, the sound of a bellowing croak.

What creature could possibly produce such a sound? None that anyone who heard it could remember seeing or hearing anywhere or anytime before. Apparently the noise was so disquieting that whenever it was heard there were mass resignations the following day, members of the household staff who were awake or had been woken by the rasping croak that came from the water.

Despite search parties being despatched on numerous occasions nothing was ever seen on, in or near the lake, although tracks of huge webbed feet were discovered on a couple of occasions, either leading to or from the perilous waters of the lake. The feet were estimated to be at least a foot wide and two feet long. No creature in Britain, none on God's Earth was known to possess such enormous feet, let alone a frog or toad.

On two occasions search parties that had been sent out to find the creature, if that is what it was, had returned a man short. It was assumed that they were dissatisfied or scared employees and that they had used the confusion to flee the confines of Tellier Hall. However, neither of the missing men took any possessions with him, and neither was ever seen or heard of again.

"Bloody hell!" exclaimed Mike. "Imagine that, being eaten by a giant toad!"

"Yeah," said Joe. "I saw a picture on the internet once of a toad in Australia and it was eating another toad, but it wasn't able to swallow it because it was too big. But it was so stupid that it wouldn't let it go. Both of them were going to die but they were just sat there with blank warty faces," here Joe pulled and impression of the toads expressions, "staring with their big googly eyes. Staring and waiting to die." He shook his head. "Weird."

"Yeah," agreed Mike thoughtfully. "It's a strange world." He paused and shook his head at the thought. "Still, doesn't sound very likely does it, a giant toad? Anyway, go on, I want to find out what happens."

Joe turned back to the text. They were nearly at the end of the queue and could see the red and black starting platform of the Vampire. They could also see the rollercoaster itself whenever it pulled in to unload one lot of riders and let on another. The front car was chiselled to a point so that it looked like a stake. Blood was splashed up the side to represent the spilled guts that came from a killed vampire.

Joe would have to read quickly if they were to finish the chapter before it was their turn to get on the rollercoaster, but it was an interesting section, the section that told of how Albert, Seventeenth Earl of Culwick had sold his soul to the devil one wild, wet and stormy night.

"Come on," said Mike, nudging Joe. "Get on with it or we'll have to stop half way through when it gets to our turn."

"Alright," said Joe, shrugging him off.

Albert, 17th Earl of Culwick, knew, well enough, the curse that was said to afflict his family; his grandfather, Gerald, had been the de Tellier found soaked to the skin with his throat cut near the gates to the estate.

That was the de Tellier, Joe realised, whose fleshless skull he had seen in the hands of the old man in the museum, the one that had sat on the desk being used as a paperweight.

Albert's father had been spared a watery death but had seen an investment in a Lancashire cotton mill literally washed away by a flash flood, and his own eldest son, Albert's older brother, had died of complications of water on the brain. Albert's father, William de Tellier, had been unable to cope with his bad luck and had turned to drink, dieing of an alcohol related illness in his forty seventh year.

A more sceptical soul may not have connected this bad luck to the curse, water on the brain is not actual water, and alcoholism is a liquid related death but not a water related one, but Albert was a superstitious man who had heard the stories of the curse night after night on the unsteady knee of his father, his boozy words blowing into the young Albert's ear and finding a home deep in the darkest corners of his mind.

The curse, if that is what it was, first reared its head when Albert was twenty two. Keenly aware that after the previous generations' disasters the family finances were not as healthy as they once had been, Albert invested in areas where he felt certain that water could not destroy his business interests. Both were on land, the first a wheat crop that he had purchased in southern England, specifically because it was far from any major rivers or sources of flooding, and secondly a rubber plantation in Malaya, selected for its sheltered location - tropical rain storms usually passed over without causing significant damage - and again there was no history of flooding.

In the first year of Albert's investment southern England enjoyed a summer of blazing temperatures and this was repeated in the second year leading to a drought and the complete failure of the wheat crop. Albert lost massively, due not to water but a lack of it. Nevertheless, his business in Malaya was doing well until the third year when an off shore earthquake caused a tsunami that rushed ashore killing a large proportion of his workforce and levelling the rubber plantation. Again, Albert lost heavily.

It was on a night not long after the terrible news from Malaya had arrived at Tellier Hall that Albert de Tellier, 17th Earl of Culwick, was sitting in an upstairs room of the house, worrying and fretting over the dire circumstances of the family finances. He had already sold off a large chunk of the estate, land that had been acquired by his ancestor Charles, the Earl who had flooded Hobsdor, after the failure of the wheat crops. In fact, the land that was sold off reduced the borders of the de Tellier estate right up to the very edge of Hobsdor Lake. Now it was possible for nosey locals to peer across the new fences that abutted Albert's land and look directly across the lake towards Tellier Hall itself.

Albert's wife had urged him to sell the land which included the lake; perhaps, she had said, with the lake gone the curse would be lifted, but Albert was of the opinion that if the curse was to be lifted then the solution lay in the lake itself and that if he gave up its ownership he would give up the control of the one thing that might redeem him from the generations of bad luck that had haunted his ancestors.

As Albert sat there that dark stormy night, trying to find a solution to his financial woes, he heard a sound that caused his scalp crawl with dread. He felt the low rumble in the wooden legs of his chair and saw the small square panes of glass in the windows tremble. Through the woods, up from the lake he heard it, the deep guttural croaking of something that had no place on this Earth or any other.

Chapter 18

Vampire

"Come on, boys, you're on," called a caped attendant with slicked back hair and white face make up. Little trickles of fake blood ran down his chin from each corner. He looked rather lame, Joe thought.

Someone in the queue behind Mike and Joe muttered at them to get a move on and after casting a snotty glance behind, the boys moved out onto the platform, Joe shoving the pamphlet into his back pocket as he went.

Their feet clanged as they made their way across the metal platform to the empty seats, three from the front, and sat down. Everything was painted black with red detail. The sound of fluttering bats, wicked laughter and terrified female screams rang out around the canopied platform stage.

A pretty young woman, made ghoulish and almost unattractive by her make-up, strapped Mike and Joe into their seats. From unseen speakers came the slow creak of a coffin opening and then a voice rang out, low, slow, sinister and foreign.

"As darkness descends my hunger awakes and so I arise, transformed into bat, rat, wolf or cat, and I begin to prowl, searching, hunting for prey, human prey. My hunger knows no limit, my craving, my desire, my lust…for blooooood! Ha ha ha hah ha!"

And they were off, the rollercoaster lurching forwards and upwards, straight up into darkness then lurching off to the right and then up again, their shoulders rattling from side to side against the seat restraints. It felt as though the cars were being pulled by something with enormous strength, up, up, upwards - and then suddenly they were outside in the uncanopied air, plummeting from a drop so huge it seemed impossible. How had they been taken so high whilst in the darkness? Their ears roared with a wind that battered at them with the speed of the drop, their lungs gasping for amazed air as slowly their stomachs, left behind at the top of the drop, caught them and squeezed back into their bellies. Then they were rushing up again, right then left, up, up, up – Joe wondered somewhere in an empty corner of his mind how the rollercoaster was driven, it seemed to gain its strength from nowhere, accelerating on inclines. It seemed impossible, jet powered. The world whipped around, pillars, metal supports, trees and then the ground rising up on the left until the sky was beneath them and then back again and around, the rumble and swoosh of the wheels on rails, the screams behind and in front, up, down, heart seeming to move within his chest, a mixture of laughter and fear trembling inside as again they careered towards the floor and almost certain destruction until whipped to the right at the last minute and then slowing to a grinding de-acceleration and then the sound of vampire laughter followed by a 'whack' 'thump' of a

112

stake hitting home and an agonised scream, mad and frustrated, rattling in their ears.

And then it was all over, they were back on the platform.

"Phew," said Mike, turning to Joe. "That was amazing."

"Best one yet," agreed Joe. "Couldn't really see what it had to do with vampires though."

They got off and checked their pictures again. This time they both looked truly petrified behind their smiles and Mike hadn't had the presence of mind to make an obscene gesture towards the camera. One of the assistants came towards the boys.

"Would you like your photo, lads?" he asked. They shook their heads. "If you change your minds you can always get an album made up at the end of the day," he smiled. "We're filming you all the time you know."

Joe and Mike's faces froze. That didn't sound good. Not good at all. That would give everything away. And why were the people at the theme park doing it? Surely that couldn't be right. Before either of the boys had a chance to speak, the assistant was talking again, rattling off his patter through a mouthful of insanely white teeth. He seemed unstoppable, like a hurricane and the boys felt almost bound to go along with whatever direction it was that he pushed them in such was his mindless enthusiasm.

"Let me show you," the assistant said. "Let me scan your bracelet." Joe reluctantly held his arm out and the assistant used a scanner to read the red plastic band that had been put around Mike's wrist when he came through the turnstile that morning.

"What happens is that we can detect your movements through scanners in the park and then use images from the cameras in those places to make a personalized film of your day in Terror Park. Isn't that neat?"

Neat? Joe considered the man with wary eyes. His skin looked too smooth and waxy, like a shop dummy's.

Sure enough, just like the man had said, as soon as the bar-code on the band had been scanned then pictures began to pop up on the television screens behind him, Joe and Mike queuing for The Styx, them arguing outside the toilet, Joe walking across the front of Tellier Hall and then down the side of the building.

"Okay, that's enough," said Joe. The man stopped the images.

"So are you interested in an album?" he asked through a smile that didn't have one tooth out of line.

"Maybe at the end," muttered Mike, pulling Joe away.

"Okey dokey," waved the man. "Have a nice stay, I mean day."

As soon as they were out of sight of the man, the boys turned to each other.

"Did you hear what he said?" asked Joe. "'Stay', not 'day'."

"Slip of the tongue?" frowned Mike

"Maybe."

"I don't like what he said about the bracelets," said Mike. "Maybe they can see us in the gardens. We're going to have to get rid of them."

"Or disable them."

"How we can do that?" asked Joe.

"We'll have to try and figure it out," said Mike, contemplating the wristband. "Maybe we can demagnetize them or something." He paused, staring at the bracelet. "Wasn't that guy a weirdo? Like a robot or a zombie."

"Yeah," replied Joe. "I bet he brushed his teeth with piss."

They both cracked up. Joe felt instantly happy, it wasn't often he was able to make Mike smile let alone laugh and after their earlier argument it made him feel more confident that Mike had forgotten about his revenge. The laughter was a release of tension, an expression of relief. Getting away from the creepy android man made both the boys realise just how uncomfortable they had been in his presence.

"Hey," said Mike, punching Joe on the arm. "Let's go and see that lake. See if we can see the church spire poking out of the water."

Joe smiled and opened the map to find out the best way there. As he did so he was conscious of the wristband touching his skin and he wondered how many pairs of eyes were watching them.

The boys decided to take the train along the narrow gauge railway whose route skirted the edge of the lake. They had spotted the station whilst consulting the map, just off in the distance, the smoke of a departing engine giving away its presence. The station certainly appeared strange, some things were too little or too low, like the track and the almost empty platform, which in turn made the shelter, the seats and the people seem too large. It was painted in black and white and the fence posts dripped with blood as though somebody had recently fallen from a great height and been impaled on them. The shelter was in the shape of a large open coffin placed on its side. A bench was within but no one was sitting on it. In fact, other than a couple in their twenties standing near the tracks and gazing into each other's eyes, Mike and Joe were the only people on the platform.

After a couple of minutes of waiting in companionable silence they heard a whistle and saw a plume of smoke rising above the hedge that bordered the track as it curved away around a corner, and then, a few moments later, the little train chuffed into view.

It wasn't a toy engine, it was a real one, the sort that had worked in and out of quarries in the first half of the twentieth century. It had a sort of foreshortened, scrunched up look to it as though too much stuff had been squeezed into too small a space. Someone had painted it black with a red funnel and a red driver's cabin, on top of which they had affixed a pair of trailing batwings.

The train disgorged most of its passengers and Mike and Joe found a couple of seats spare in one of the three open sided wooden carriages. They slid onto the slatted wooden seats that opened on either side without any door or guard. Joe guessed that the train didn't go very fast as there was nothing to stop a person from falling out.

The two boys grinned. Although this wasn't really a ride, and it was incredibly tame, almost childish or nerdy, they were both excited, not that either of them would have admitted it. Perhaps it was the fact that they knew that the tracks would take them along the banks of Lake Hobsdor - the place where the de Telliers' ill-fortune and the curse originated - that made them so excited at the prospect of their journey.

With a sudden blast of its whistle and then a sharp tug and jerk forward of the carriages, the train was on its way. First it ran around the back of The Vampire, its huge arching track soaring across the sky to the left like some gargantuan fossilized serpent, and then it passed what Joe realised was the back of the old house, Tellier Hall. The thought of the strange figure in the upstairs room that wasn't actually there flitted through his mind.

The line ran under trees and they realised that they were entering the ornamental gardens. Now that the trees and the verges and valleys shielded them from the noise of the park, all they could hear was the steady click of the carriage wheels on the rail joins and the busy puffing of the locomotive up ahead.

"I wonder if this is near our spot," whispered Joe leaning forward, even though there was nobody to overhear.

"Reckon so," nodded Mike. "Must be."

The oily smell of the train and its smuts mixed with heady wafts of pollen from the clouds of flowers that clustered on the banks of the cuttings.

After a minute or so in the woods there came a sudden rumble and looking down Mike and Joe saw they were on a wooden viaduct crossing a foaming stream twenty five feet below. To the right of the bridge was a steep wall covered in moss and at least thirty feet high, so high that it rose up above the level of the track. The stream was emerging from a hole in the base of the wall and gushing under the bridge and onto the rocks.

"Wouldn't want to fall out here!" shouted Mike over the noise of the rumbling wheels and water. Joe nodded, beaming.

And suddenly they were out of the tree cover and under the big blue sky and blazing sun. Both boys simultaneously raised their hands to shield their eyes from the glare of the light reflecting off the lake.

"Wow!" said Mike. "And there's a *village* down there?"

"Used to be. Nobody knows how much is left now."

Before long the train shut off steam and cruised silently into a little halt with a wooden platform and shelter. There had been no attempt to make it look scary, it just looked rustically simple, almost twee.

Mike and Joe were the only passengers to get off the train. Mike ran forwards to the head of the train to speak to the driver before he set off again.

"How often do the trains stop?" he asked.

"Every fifteen minutes on the lake loop," answered the moustachioed engineer, wiping his oily hands on filthy blue overalls. Mike thanked the man and stepped back as the driver prepared to depart.

The train pulled out in huffing plumes of white blue smoke and the boys watched as it made its slow way around the lake. Eventually they could barely make out the red of the engine and could only follow its progress by the line of dissolving smoke, and then that too disappeared as the track disappeared into some trees.

The boys turned, Mike strolling towards the shelter to examine something he had seen inside the structure.

"Bloody hell!" he said after a moment. "Come and look at this."

Joe looked at where Mike was pointing, it was the sign for the station. 'Beast Feeder Halt' it read.

Joe and Mike looked at each other and raised their eyebrows, neither one sure how to react to the name.

"And look at this," said Joe, pointing towards the simple wooden shelter of the railway halt. Inside was a hand carved picture depicting a creature with bulging eyes and a wide mouth lined with jagged teeth. The animal - a toad - was shown crawling from water, and yet it could not possibly be a toad for just in front of the creature, cowering on the foreshore, was a horse, dwarfed and tiny beside the hideous bulk of the advancing monstrosity.

"Looks like a toad with teeth," said Mike, mirroring Joe's thoughts. "Toads don't have teeth do they?""

"No," said Joe. "I don't think any amphibians do, you know, frogs and newts. Maybe it's like a crocodile or something, a reptile."

"Yeah, maybe!" snorted Mike. "Who are you all of a sudden, a bloody biology teacher? Maybe it never existed at all. Did that occur to you? Maybe it's crawled out the mind of a man who's had too much whisky."

Joe sniffed in a dignified manner and pretended to ignore Mike.

Underneath the carving was a metal plaque affixed to the wall. The boys inclined their heads to read what it said.

It is from this point in 1924, that park gamekeeper, Edward Spry, claims to have seen a huge creature emerge from the water on the opposite shore of the lake and devour a young pony. The engraving above is based on a sketch

119

that Spry made for his employer, Michael de Tellier, 20th Earl of Culwick..

While many at the time did not believe Edward Spry's story, a pony - the Earl's daughter's - was found to be missing on the night of the gamekeeper's supposed encounter and was never recovered. Some claim that Spry knew of the legend surrounding Hobsdor Lake and made up the tale of the toad beast as cover for a confederate who was engaged in the theft of the pony on the other side of the lake.

Others believe that such a beast exists in the lake to this day.

"Yeah, right," scoffed Mike. "That sounds *really* likely."

"It fits with the curse," said Joe.

"I can believe in a curse," said Mike. "But a massive toad living in the lake and eating horses! Come *on*!"

Joe shrugged and stepped off the platform and across the tracks. Mike followed him and they walked down to the water's edge. Tiny waves lapped at the mud that stretched from the grass and extended down to the water for a couple of feet.

"You can see it's been a hot summer," said Joe, pointing. "Look how much water is missing from the lake."

"Yeah," replied Mike. "Perhaps we can hear the church bells." He was serious now.

Both boys were silent, straining to listen, but all they could hear were the whoops, yells and rattle of the rides that drifted over the water from the theme park.

"Come on," said Mike, sitting down. "Read me the bit about that prat selling his soul to the devil."

"Okay," said Joe, grinning as he pulled the leaflet from his back pocket and sat down next to Mike.

As Albert sat there that dark stormy night, trying to find a solution to his financial woes, he heard a sound that caused his scalp crawl with dread. He felt the low rumble in the wooden legs of his chair and saw the small square panes of glass in the windows tremble. Through the woods, up from the lake he heard it, the deep guttural croaking of something that had no place on this Earth or any other.

The Earl knew what the sound signified, and despite the flesh of his arms and his back crawling in a chilly revulsion he knew that something must be done and it had to be done now. He knew that if it was not done then someone from among his family, perhaps he himself, would lie cold and dead before the sun came again to shine on the surface of the Earth twenty four hours hence.

Albert's Uncle George had been a keen believer the occult - matters of magic and devil worship that is - and when he had died, peacefully of a winter virus that had taken him at the age of fifty eight, he had bequeathed Albert his library of occult books.

Until that evening Albert had rarely thought of them let alone opened them, but on this darkest of nights he realised that if no solutions to his troubles lay upon the Earth then perhaps they lay somewhere beyond. And so it was that with heavy heart Albert, 17th Earl of Culwick found himself trailing a finger along the bookshelves until, as though led to a particular spot, he stopped and pulled a dusty, red, leather bound volume from the shelf, a volume that he had never before noticed, a volume by one Arturio Montmorencey entitled, *Summoning the Great Powers of Beelzebub, Lucifer, Lord of the Underworld and all Other Titles by Which His Satanic Majesty Might be Known, and Methods Thereafter by Which He Might be Returned to His Kingdom of Infinite Darkness.*

"Catchy title," interrupted Mike. Joe ignored him and carried on.

Albert suddenly recalled a tale told to him many dim years before, a tale told by his Uncle George of how the book had been bound in the skin of a man hanged for stealing a lamb. Albert had never believed his uncle, had never wanted to believe that the dry leather that clothed the boards of the book had once lain supple and smooth, warm with life on the body of a living breathing young man. Tonight with the volume in his hands he was not so sure that the story was not, after all, true.

Inside Albert read of how one might summon the Devil from Hell and how a deal might be done with him whereby the soul of a man might be given in exchange for any favour on Earth, riches and fame and all that a human being might desire. But when that human being reached the end of his or her time on this meagre planet they would know that all they had achieved was for nothing, that all must be left behind, for nothing can be taken into the land of the dead, and for the man with no soul, the man who had traded his soul for the riches of the living, the land of the dead that he must travel to is Hell and it is in Hell for ever and ever and ever that he must live, a slave to the Devil, paying back a debt that can never be repaid. Satan, as all good God fearing folk know, charges a terrible rate of interest.

The Earl knew all of this, knew that should he sell his soul he would be damned and that nothing could save him from a destiny in Hell, but he was prepared to sacrifice himself, even if it meant for all eternity.

The Earl was not a greedy man, it was not for himself that he wished to gain favours, it was for his family, for all his descendants who would otherwise be cursed; Albert was sacrificing himself for his family.

How do we know all this? Because the Earl wrote it all down in his diary that very same night.

The leaflet described how Albert collected the necessary items to perform the ritual ("What items?" asked Mike in frustration) and made his way to the edge of the lake. Once there he performed the ritual, the details of which and the items used were not revealed; Albert did not want any to follow in his wicked footsteps, and later he burnt the book, the volume bound with human skin. As he did so, he reported, the smoke that curled up formed itself into the shape of a howling bloody boy who then dissolved into the bitter night air.

What the Earl does reveal, however, is that the ceremony worked, that the devil did indeed appear on the shores of Lake Hobsdor.

From the centre of the lake came a dreadful sucking sound. The Earl made out movement on the inky surface of the waters. He realised with an awed dread that slowly the water was starting to turn, was beginning to revolve in an anti-clockwise direction, growing faster and faster, and as it did so the terrible whooshing sound that flew across the water towards him grew louder and the sucking sound grew deeper and more dreadful. It was like the last ghastly exhalation of some enormous beast, an unearthly death rattle.

In the middle of the lake the swirling water was dipping into a cone, creating a whirlpool. The sound was so huge, so unearthly and terrifying that the Earl records that he was struck with mortal fear and almost turned and ran. He also records that he wished he had paid heed to these instincts and thus saved his everlasting soul from the eternity of torments that he believed awaited him after death.

Just as he was backing away, just as he was on the verge of turning and fleeing, he saw it, the shape that was emerging from the base of the whirlpool. It started as a spike, a ragged line jutting from the water, still, motionless in the surrounding torrent. As the whirlpool grew deeper and more of the spike was revealed the Earl realised that it was the spire of a church poking out of the water, the crooked and jagged remains of its crucifix still partially intact at the top, pointing upwards like a blasphemous finger jabbing at heaven.

As the water receded further the Earl could make out something clinging to the spire and when it moved, slowly and huge, he realised that it was a figure, a lithe muscular figure, massive and smooth, a centre of darkness in the midnight hour. The figure began to stretch itself upwards and revealed the full enormity of its height and build. Slowly it turned its head and as it did so it revealed burning red pinpricks in the blackness, burning eyes that locked onto his, coals of angry fire.

The Earl's bones felt weak in his legs and he staggered looking for support, unsure that his mind or his body could bear to accept the horror of what he was seeing. In his soul he felt a tearing, a horrible realisation that what he had done was wrong and could never be put right. His mouth muttered silent prayers to a God above who was no longer listening. With fear for his life and soul, the Earl tried to run but found that he was unable, his feet were locked to the ground, held as though by quicksand.

It was at that moment that the figure sprang from the spire in a motion so fluid and powerful that he covered in one bound a distance twice that of a football pitch. Upon landing on the surface of the lake the figure did not splash or submerge but sprang forward again and began running across the water itself, feet touching on the surface making the tiniest of ripples and faintest of sounds. But of these tiny sounds there were many, as his feet struck the surface, as his massive legs lunged forwards and then pushed backwards in huge strides towards the Earl.

Petrified, frozen as though hypnotized, Albert, 17th Earl of Culwick could do nothing but watch as the fearsome sight of Satan, Prince of Darkness and Lord of Hell strode purposefully from off the water and up the shore to where he had collapsed.

The Devil stood towering over him, eight feet tall, his head smooth and bald, beads of glittering water running down his brow and over his terrible face, and the muscular contours of his body, a handsome statue of cold chiselled power.

Behind the boys a whistle blew and they turned to see a train approaching the station. It stopped but no one got off. The driver waved to the boys and they waved back. The whistle blew again and the little red train pulled slowly away in a cloud of steam.

Sitting in the rear carriage sat the old man from the museum, but Joe had not noticed. The old man was smiling and stroking the soft burlap bag that he held in his lap.

"Bloody Hell," said Mike, staring out across the lake. "Remind me never to call up the devil."

"Hmm", replied Joe. A shiver had just run his spine but he had no idea why.

After the train had gone Joe began reading again. There was no description of what took place between the Devil and the Earl, only that the deal was struck; that in return for the soul of the Earl the Devil would lift the curse that had lain upon the de Tellier family for all those years.

The Earl records that Satan then crossed his arms about his chest and with a hideous grin of triumph the ground beneath him opened up and he slid without a sound feet first into the silty earth at the shore's edge. His eyes remained fixed on the Earl's until the sand covered his open eyeballs and for a moment only the surface of his huge bald head remained visible in the sand like the stump of some huge mutilated limb, and then it too disappeared.

The Earl then records that he was unable to sleep for three days after his strange meeting.

Joe stopped reading.

"There's one more chapter," he said. "Do you want me to carry on?"

Mike looked at his watch.

"Bloody hell, it's nearly four thirty," he exclaimed. "We need to get on a ride quick. They'll be kicking out in an hour and a half."

"Yeah, and we've still got to get back to the other side of the lake," added Joe, standing up and dusting down the seat of his jeans.

"What are we going to do?" said Mike, peering down the line. "How long ago do you think that train went past?"

Joe looked at his watch.

"Can't have been less than five minutes. How often did the driver say they went?"

"I think it was fifteen minutes. We might as well wait", replied Mike. "Unless you fancy swimming across."

Joe looked at him and was glad to see that he was joking. The thought of sleeping in the woods was bad enough without the thought of a strange creature living in the lake, even if he did know that it couldn't possibly exist. And as for the Devil, well that didn't bear thinking about even if he didn't believe in the Devil and God and that sort of thing.

The boys walked up to the platform and stood peering at the woods to their right, searching for the tell tale line of cotton wool looping up out of the tree tops. Mike soon got bored and before Joe could stop him he had picked up a stone and was carving something in the sign that announced the station's name.

"What are you doing?" Joe shouted, outraged by Mike's act of vandalism, and gave him a push.

Mike gave him a sly, stupid grin and stepped away. Joe couldn't stop himself from grinning. Now, instead of saying 'Beast Feeder Halt', the sign said 'Breast Feeder Halt'.

Before either of them could say anything a whistle sounded in the distance. They turned to look and saw the train emerging from the trees.

"About time," said Mike.

The ride back around the lake in the opposite direction wasn't as interesting, it just skirted the lake and then ran through some hedges and into the theme park again. The boys were not taking much notice of the view, they were more interested in looking at the map and trying to decide which ride they had the best chance of getting on before they stopped taking people into the queues and then started chucking them out of the park. They knew they'd have to make their way to their hiding place while there were still plenty of people around. Two boys running around in a near empty park would be noticed immediately.

Chapter 19

End of Day

Mike and Joe decided to take a ride on The Lair of the White Worm which was a disappointment, spinning around in the darkness and flashing a few multi-coloured lights while a recording of some actresses screaming played in the background. That was why there had only been a short queue.

The boys were so disgusted with their choice that they didn't even comment on it as they emerged into the dazzling afternoon light, just made their way to the park exit. Not that it was the exit for them, they were just after their bags.

It was gone five forty and though neither boy said it out loud, they were both nervous. Streams of people were now heading for the exit. Once they had got their bags from the lockers they would look conspicuous walking towards the gardens against the flow of the crowds. Joe could see Mike's mouth was pursed and his brow furrowed. They both walked a little faster.

It was five forty nine by Mike's watch by the time they got to the lockers. Joe fetched his bag from his own locker and turned to see Mike, a look of panic on his face, rummaging in his pockets. He couldn't find his key. After turning out all of his pockets twice he accused Joe of having it. Joe didn't bother arguing despite being sure he hadn't got it, he knew how Mike could get at these moments and knew that it was pointless getting into a debate. Mike was sweating and jittery and looking for someone to blame. Joe was the only one there so Mike wanted it to be his fault. Rather than say anything, Joe let his actions speak and silently emptied all of his pockets to reveal some money, his phone and some gum. Mike swore and ran his hands through his hair.

"Bollocks! We're running out of time. Where could it have gone?"

"It must have fallen out on one of the rides."

"Yeah, probably the one where you were messing around," spat Mike. Joe had known that Mike would bring that up now that he alone was responsible for losing his key. Mike was like that, he could never just take the blame for his own mistakes. It was what Joe found most irritating about Mike.

"Look," said Joe. "If you've lost a key on the rides then loads of other people must have done the same thing at some point. Go and ask that bloke over there," he said, pointing to a bored looking man slumped in a chair under a 'Help Point' sign. He was watching the departing crowds with a disinterested gaze.

Mike frowned. "What if this takes ages? We might not be able to get back to the gardens, they might chuck us out."

"If you do it *now* there might still be time. What else can we do?"

Mike growled and stamped his foot before reluctantly making his way over to the uniformed man. Joe watched him explaining his plight. The man's expression didn't change, he just got up and walked across to the lockers, fishing in his pockets for a large bunch of keys as he came.

He tried a couple, humming as he did so, until he found one that opened Mike's locker.

"You're going to have to tell me what I'm going to find in here if you want it," the man said.

"A black Puma bag, a holdall," stuttered Mike, his face flushing red.

The man opened the door and pulled out Mike's bag.

"And now you're going to have to tell me what I'm going to find in here," he said, glancing up at Mike from his squatting position.

Mike turned even redder.

"What do you mean? That's private. You can't look in there."

The man's expression, if anything, grew more bored.

"If you can't tell me what's inside then how do I know it's yours, huh? Anyone can watch a person put a bag in a locker and then tell me that they've lost their key. They've seen the bag being put in the locker, it's easy for them to describe it. What they can't say what's inside it. You want the bag, you tell me what's inside."

Joe could see Mike tussling with himself, trying to make a decision. He realised that Mike didn't want the man to see what he had, if he did he might realise that they had a plan to stay in the park overnight, some of the equipment was a giveaway. Joe started to feel annoyed at Mike for jeopardising their plan.

"Just tell him," he snapped.

Mike looked angrily back at Joe and then told the man what was in it, a torch, a sleeping bag, a jumper and a coat among other things. The man's expression didn't change, he didn't care. He wasn't bothered what the boys were up to just so long as he got the right bag back to the right person. Joe could tell all this as Mike was agitatedly running through the contents. The man slowly opened the bag and checked it before handing it over to Mike.

"Thank you," said Mike, looking to see if the man was going to say anything but he just nodded and sucked his teeth without looking at either boy. Slowly he rose to his feet and walked away back to his chair, wiping his hands on his trousers as he went as though touching the bag had made his fingers dirty.

Mike looked at his watch. It was five fifty nine.

"Crap," he said. "We'll never make it. We'll get caught."

Joe had already started running. "Come on," he called back. "Hurry up."

He slowed slightly to allow Mike to catch up. "It's easy," Joe said. "If someone stops us we'll tell them we're going back to get your mobile. You left it in that Blood Burger, remember?"

It took Mike a moment to cotton on.

"Oh yeah," he said, breaking into a relieved grin.

"And that's why we're running," Joe went on. "So that we can get it and then get back to the exit before they close the doors."

"Oh yeah," grinned Mike and sprinted ahead of Joe. "Come on then you old woman, what are you waiting for?"

No one stopped them or even glanced at them as they ran to the ornamental garden. Joe noticed a couple of the CCTV cameras that the man at the photo shop had mentioned but he thought that it was unlikely they'd be a problem. They were only for people who wanted to buy a picture. If you didn't turn in your bracelet so that it could be scanned in order to make up film of your day, then the park shouldn't even notice you on the CCTV footage. They wouldn't be looking for you, surely.

But then a horrible thought occurred to Joe. What if the bracelets were scanned as you exited through the turnstiles? What then if at the end of the day their computers flagged up any bracelets that hadn't passed through the turnstiles and the scanners? They would surely assume that the wearers were still in the park. Couldn't they then look on the CCTV, checking through the images to see where you might be? Wouldn't they then come looking? Perhaps they could track you down with some kind of detection device.

"Stop," he yelled to Mike.

Mike skidded to a halt. His chest was rising and falling with the exertion of their run. They were standing at a fork in the path. One way led into the ornamental gardens, the other skirted the outside and was signposted as heading for the 3D cinemas. Joe was pretty sure that this particular way

135

into the gardens was the same way they'd entered before. He hoped Mike knew.

"What is it?" Mike hissed back.

"Your bracelet, the wristband, we've got to take them off," panted Joe.

"Why?"

"Just do it. There isn't time to discuss it." He was right. It was eight minutes past six, the last people would be leaving the park and they would have no business to be where they were any more, they had to get out of sight. Joe whipped off his bag and dug around inside until he found his Swiss Army Knife.

The bracelets were made of non-tearable rubber and were too tight to slip over the wrist. Joe opened the sharpest blade of his knife and hacked off his and then Mike's wristband, then he picked them up from where they had fallen on the tarmac path and hurled them into a nearby bush.

"Go on then," he said to Mike. "You lead." After a brief nod Mike took off again, down the path that led into the gardens. Joe shouldered his bag and headed after him, his breath not quite recovered from the first bout of running.

Before he left the path and entered the dense woodland of the ornamental gardens Joe took a last clear look at the pale blue sky.

It was ten past six when they finally flopped down in their hiding place in the hollow centre of the flowering bush. They weren't out of breath as they hadn't run the last bit, Joe had slowed them down and they had carefully made their way down the winding paths being sure to be as silent as possible. They passed no one and before they had left the path to enter the foliage behind which their hideout lay they had stopped and listened until they were certain that no one was following. Then, quiet with stealth, they had vanished into the sculpted undergrowth.

Lying on their backs, staring up through the leaves at the darkening blue of the early evening sky, the boys were attacked by a fit of the giggles, they had done it, they were in their hide and no one had seen them. Mission accomplished. They were seized by the delicious thrill that comes of knowing that you are doing something forbidden, that you are getting one over on someone powerful and that they don't even know it. They had to stifle their laughter, there were still three hours of daylight left and plenty of time for them to get caught, but both of the boys knew exactly what it was that the other was laughing at. They were laughing at their own audacity.

Chapter 20

Silent Communication

Joe had brought a little sketch book with him, he took it everywhere he went, stuck into the back pocket of his jeans along with a stubby HB pencil. His one and only talent, he thought, was an ability to render lifelike images of plants and animals on paper. It was something he loved to do, something calm amidst the insanity and bustle of everyday life, and something that brought peace to his busy and often worried mind. It was the one thing that made the world stop and his breathing slow. Joe hadn't thought that there would be much time to sketch at Terror Park, but he was glad that he had brought the book anyway as it now meant that he and Mike could talk without speaking.

It hadn't occurred to either of them that they might have to be silent for a long time, that even whispering might give the game away. It was very quiet in the gardens and every tiny sound seemed to magnify itself and fill the surrounding air. Just opening the zip on Joe's bag seemed to announce their presence to every park attendant for a thousand yards around.

The first thing that Mike wrote was, *wot do we do if we need da toilet?*

They had both started giggling again.

No 1 or no 2? Joe wrote and that had made it even worse.

They came up with an answer though, they would hold it in for as long as possible and if they did have to go – number ones only – then they would go in the far corner where the ground was slightly lower, and then wash it away with a little drinking water. Number twos were strictly off limits.

They chatted using the note pad for a while, enjoying the novelty of it, but after half an hour they were beginning to grow bored. Joe wondered if they'd have it in them to stay still and patient all evening, he doubted it. Then he remembered *The Curse of the de Tellier Family* pamphlet that was folded it up in his pocket. They still hadn't read the last chapter, the one that brought matters up to the present day.

He fished it out of his back pocket and showed it to Mike who nodded enthusiastically. Joe opened it to the right page and then spread it on the ground. Both boys lay on their stomachs, heads side by side and began to read.

They had only just started when a sound made them look up and their hearts contract, footfalls and the low murmur of male conversation. The crunch of heavy boots on gravel drew nearer.

Joe was holding his breath and straining so hard to be silent that he could hear his own heart pumping and the blood in his ears hissing its way around the blood vessels that followed the delicate contours.

The men were talking about football he realised, Manchester United and Valencia, apparently there was a game on the TV that night. They both hated Manchester United for some reason and were desperate that Valencia should win. Then, almost as suddenly as they had appeared, the men's voices faded and the crunch of their boots drew further away until eventually nothing could be heard.

Joe let his breath out in a low whistle of release. Mike did likewise. They looked at each other and grinned, then turned back to reading.

All was well for Albert and his family for the next thirty years. By that time Albert was an elderly man, but his eldest son was still young enough to be serving in the army at the rank of captain. It was 1916 and World War I was raging across Europe.

Although the luck of the de Tellier family had been good for the past three decades and the sound of the toad had not been heard, Albert de Tellier was still wary of tempting fate and had instructed his son, Evelyn, to enlist in the army rather than pursue the naval career that he had so desired. Evelyn, an obedient son who was aware of the substantial inheritance awaiting him if he played by the rules did as he was asked. He was probably aware of his two younger brothers, Edward and Paul, peering eagerly over his shoulder, hungry for their own slice of the pie. Both boys had also taken up commissions in the army, Edward serving in the relative safety of the British protectorate of Southern Africa, and Paul as an early member of the Royal Flying Corps who was presently notching up an impressive number of 'kills' in his Sopwith Strutter over the Western Front.

Edward, a fluent speaker of German, was not, in fact, in quite the safe position that he had led his family to believe. Due to his linguist abilities he was often dispatched to the nearby German colony of Cameroon, the part that later became the British protectorate of South Cameroon, on 'fact finding missions'. This was a polite way of saying that he was involved in spying and sabotage against German targets.

What none of them knew was that the de Tellier luck was about to take a definite turn for the worse.

It was a cold October day when an elderly man, not much younger than the Earl himself, appeared at the gates of Tellier Hall and requested a meeting with the Earl on 'a matter of some urgency'. The Earl, curious as to the nature of the man's business, agreed to see him and the man was brought into the scullery of the Hall where the Earl duly met him.

The man explained that he had his son's mortal remains upon his person, in the knapsack which he carried upon his back, and that his son had been killed lately at the Battle of Loos. It was his son's peculiar desire, the man said, which he had expressed before departing for France, that should he be killed and his body recovered, his remains be laid to rest alongside his ancestors in the graveyard of Hobsdor Church.

At the mention of Hobsdor Church the Earl's blood ran cold. Did the man realise, he asked, that the church lay beneath more than thirty fathoms of water? Indeed he did, the man replied, and all that he asked was that his son's remains be weighted and dropped from a boat in the centre of the Lake, as closely approximating the location of the church as possible. The man had heard, he said, that the church's spire could, in summers of drought, be seen from the shore.

At these words the Earl shivered. Bemused by the man's request the Earl asked the man how it could be that he carried his son's mortal remains in his knapsack which was nought but a small canvas bag. Wordlessly the man removed his bag from his shoulder, opened it and produced a bandaged bundle.

"Here within, Sir," he said, "lies my son's left arm." His son's trench, he explained, had been hit by a German shell and nothing further of his son had been recovered. The boy's identity, or rather the identity of the arm, had only been possible due to a friend of the unfortunate son's recognising his signet ring and wristwatch, both of which were still attached to the limb, the wristwatch still ticking.

After a moment's reflection the Earl had explained to the man that his request was out of the question. What if the weights came loose? He couldn't have a decomposing arm floating to the surface or washing up on the shore, and besides, it seemed highly unlikely that it was a legal form of burial.

The man looked at the Earl with cold grey eyes. He stared at him motionless - impertinently, the Earl thought at the time - and then leaned towards the Earl and whispered in his ear.

At once the colour drained from the Earl's face and as the man backed away, still holding his gaze, and until he turned on his heel and walked out of the scullery, the Earl remained where he was, utterly dumbstruck, his face a picture of horror. In his right hand he still held the piece of paper that his butler had given him informing him of the man's name. Snapping from the trance into which he had fallen, the Earl looked down at the folded piece of paper. So certain had he been that the man was not a person of consequence, the Earl had not even bothered to look at the fellow's name. Slowly he unfolded the paper and looked down at the two words written there, bold and plain. Edgar Trundle.

"Trundle?" whispered Mike, pointing at the name on the page. "Wasn't that..."

"Yes," said Joe. "The same name as the woman who cursed the thirteenth Earl when he was about to drown the village to make Hobsdor Lake." Joe was several paragraphs ahead of Mike and had to keep waiting for him to catch up before he could turn the page.

"That's a bit of a coincidence isn't it? Too much of a coincidence I'd say," said Mike.

"Well obviously," hissed Joe. "It must have been one of her descendents."

"And what did Edgar Trundle say to the Earl?"

"How should I know?" replied Joe, jabbing the page and turning the page. "Read faster!"

Since the two men had walked past earlier the boys hadn't heard anything further apart from the sounds of creatures in the undergrowth and birds in the trees. Nevertheless, thinking of the men made Mike remember something.

"Damn! We didn't use the dog spray!"

"Shush!" hissed Joe.

"But I haven't sprayed the dog repellent," said Mike irritably.

"Well, do it quickly and do it quietly," replied Joe.

Mike was making a lot of noise rummaging in his bag and Joe was worried about the attention they might be attracting with their stage whispered conversation. Mike finally located the spray and had it in his hand. He crouched by the little hole in the bush that led to the trail they had found from the path. He turned back towards Joe.

"Where do you think I should spray it?"

"You're going to have to do it where we came off the path or otherwise a dog could lead the guards to the trail and if they follow that, it'll lead them here. It's not an obvious trail but if they realise it's there then it won't be hard to follow, will it?"

Mike pulled a face, he'd obviously hoped that Joe would say just to do it outside the bush.

"Do you want me to go?" asked Joe.

Mike shook his head. There was no way he was going to let

Joe make him look like a chicken. He took a deep breath and squeezed through the hole. The branches and leaves crackled with a terrible volume, one that they hadn't noticed when they'd come in.

Joe wriggled over to the hole on his belly. He could hear Mike's progress and decided that if a noise was being made he might as well watch Mike and watch out for him at the same time. By moving on his belly again Joe made almost no noise and was soon crouched outside the bush, peering over an ugly sprawled plant with wide purple flowers. Why couldn't Mike have moved like this, thought Joe, and then he realised that he wouldn't have wanted to get any muck on his precious Adidas T-shirt.

Looking down from his vantage point Joe had a fairly good view of Mike as he reached the path.

The evening light had gradually changed and amber beams slanted through the leaves and branches of the overarching trees, darkening the colours and softening the edges of the plants.

Although he told himself it was stupid and that no one could hear his breathing, Joe still took shallow intakes of air. What made it all the more absurd was that he and everyone who might have happened to be in the near vicinity could hear every little noise that Mike was making, in the silence everything was magnified. Joe could even hear a small insect whining in his ear and had to fight the urge to violently slap at it.

Mike reached the end of the trail and was crouching at the edge of the path looking left and then right and then back again, apparently unsure if his coast was clear.

"GO!" hissed Joe as loudly as he dared. He was sure that at any moment someone would appear and that they would see Mike making his way back up the trail.

Mike looked back at him angrily, finger held to his lips, and then he made his way out onto the path. He started spraying the ground in a haphazard manner, waving his extended arm to and fro. The loud hiss of the aerosol made Joe wince, how could anyone not hear such a noise in the still of the gardens? If only they had done it when they had got there. Mike backed away towards the trail, still spraying and then started walking backwards up the trail itself, the aerosol spluttering and farting as it began running out, and then, with a last squirting blow, it was gone. Mike shook it and there was a rattle, but before he could do another thing, he froze in mid shake, his arm poised.

Joe froze too, his breathing caught between inhalation and exhalation.

There it was, unmistakable, two voices and the crackle of a walkie talkie, footsteps hurrying towards them.

Hurrying.

Running.

Mike looked back at Joe, his face a white mask of panic, desperate for advice, for help, but Joe could think of absolutely nothing that could save Mike from discovery.

Chapter 21

Capture

Mike started running, keeping low and bouncing from the toes of one foot to the toes of the other to minimise the noise he made but still there was rustling and crackling as he hurtled along the trail.

Joe started to back through the hole as quickly and quietly as he could, making space for Mike to get through and back into the cover of the bush. He was pretty sure that the men's voices had stopped, but wasn't sure if he couldn't hear them over the noise that he and Mike were making. Perhaps they had heard the noise of the shaking foliage and had stopped, listening.

Then Joe heard the crackle of the men's walkie talkie and realised that he was right, they had stopped talking.

Mike's feet suddenly shot through the gap as he tried to slide back into the hideout, but then found himself unable to push himself through. Joe grabbed his ankles and pulled. Mike suddenly appeared, his T-shirt rucked up to expose his white stomach and thin, rib lined chest. His face was pale and his eyes wide. He was breathing heavily.

Joe flopped down next to him and held an urgent finger up to his lips. There was almost silence, just the ragged intake and exhalation of Mike's breathing. Even the birds who had been making something of a twilight chorus had fallen silent.

The sound of the men's footsteps grew louder and then a burst of static broke the quiet and an electronic voice, gravelled with static, spoke with a Geordie accent. The boys couldn't hear what it said but they heard the reply.

"Not sure. Over. There's nothing here but we'll take a closer look. Could just have been an animal. Over."

Then the walkie talkie again, though this time they could understand it.

"Let us know if you find anything. Over. Do you require assistance? Over. I could get a scanner or a dog with you in ten minutes. Over."

'Please no, please no, please no', the boys repeated in their heads.

"That won't be necessary, over. Pretty sure it was an animal, over. We'll let you know if we need any help. Over and out." The boys heard a switch being clicked and then the voice of a second man.

"What does he think we're going to find, Lord Lucan or the Loch Ness monster? Terrorists trying to get a couple of free rides?"

"It's Jackson, you know what he's like. Takes everything too seriously. Boring job, boring life. Anything to make his day a bit more exciting."

"We've got boring jobs but we don't think we're in the SAS do we."

149

"He's been told there've been people sleeping in the gardens. He's personally insulted by that. He wants to be the one to catch them."

The boys' hearts froze. Were they on to them? It was shocking to think that they weren't the first people to have their idea, they'd been certain it was such a good ruse that no one had thought of it before. It had never occurred to them that if it was such a good idea then lots of other people might have thought of it before.

"Do you think it's true?" said the second man. "You know, people sleeping overnight?"

"Dunno", said the first. "Apparently the gardeners have found evidence of people sleeping rough, but that could have been left by people in the day as far as I can tell, you know school teachers sneaking off for a peaceful snooze, teenagers looking for somewhere to have a bit of a fumble."

The second man laughed.

"Sounded like an animal to me, crashing about like that. We probably startled a badger, something about that size."

Joe stifled a giggle. He had realised what Mike's nickname was going to be from now on. Badger. A sudden pain flashed in his right arm as a furious Mike punched him. It was as though Mike had read Joe's mind, but he was just angry at the noise Joe had made. But by punching Joe, Mike had made even more noise.

From down on the path there came a sniffing sound and then the voice of the second man again.

"Funny smell though, don't you think? Kind of…chemical smell."

150

"Yeah", agreed the first man. "But also…what is it? Black Jacks? Liquorice? Aniseed? That's it, aniseed."

"Isn't that what badger piss smells like?"

The two men laughed.

"Come on," said the first man. "This is a waste of time. Let's get back. The first half has already started."

"You better let Jackson know there's nothing here or he'll be sending in a SWAT team."

The sound of the men's voices moved away with the sound of their feet. When they had gone and silence had returned Mike let out a sigh of relief.

"Phew, that was lu…"

Joe put a finger to his lips and reached for his sketchbook. He scribbled something down and showed it to Mike.

No mre talkin, only writin.

Mike nodded and pantomimed wiping sweat from his forehead. They both realised that they'd had a very lucky escape.

Fink deyl b bk? Wrote Joe.

Ope not, wrote Mike.

If dey bring dogz we shd b ok, bt if dey find da braclets in da bush dey mite realise were in ere, Joe scribbled.

NE1 cud ave don dat. Dey cud ave jus gt fed up wif wearin dem. Dsnt mean sum1z inside da woodz asleep.

'Spose,' Joe replied. *Bt wot bout ppl sleepin in da gardenz b4. If sum1 as used dis spot dey mite cum n chek it agen. Did it lk like som1 ad bin ere b4?*

Na, bt da trail wuz der, sum1 ad usd dat b4. Stop worryin. Wotz da wrst dat cn appen 2 us? Dey catch us – so wot? Dey cn only throw us out da park cnt dey? NEway, were only kidz. Deyd av 2 look afta us.

'Spose', wrote Joe, and that was when his phone started ringing. He scrabbled at his pocket and as he pulled it out the sound became louder as the material of his jeans stopped muffling it. In his alarm he fumbled it, failing to find the keypad. It rang three more times before he managed to switch it off. There was an ominous silence.

"You bloody div," hissed Mike.

"Shhh."

"It's a bit late for that isn't it."

Silence. Something moved in the undergrowth and a confused bird made a strangulated chirping high in a tree. Joe wrote something on the pad and Mike squinted to see. It was starting to get dark.

Dey'll fink it wuz 1 of der fonez.

Mike took the pen and wrote savagely, the pen nearly tearing the paper.

Ud beta ope so.

Joe grabbed the pen off him.

Ave U trnd YUR fone off???

Mike read the message and was motionless, his eyes pointedly refusing to look at Joe, then he dug in his pocket for his phone.

Joe rolled over so that Mike was at his back, and took his own phone back out of his pocket. He switched it on again and listened to the message. It was a voicemail from his mum. She never used text language, she didn't know how.

"Hello Joe," her voice rang out merrily. "Are you alright? Hope you're having fun. Give us a call when you get this. Dad sends his love." There was a brief pause, then, "It's Mum." As if he wouldn't know. And then, "Love you."

Joe started texting a message in reply. Mike hit him in the back.

"The light'll attract them."

"Piss off. I'll just be a minute."

'I'm okay. Having fun. Love you both. See you tomorrow,' Joe texted in standard English. If he texted as he normally did his mum wouldn't have a clue what he was saying. He felt a terrible pang at lying to his mum and wished he was at home in his living room watching the telly with her next to him, his dad in his armchair reading his paper, and his dog, Alfie, asleep at his feet. The thought that Mike might still want to get his revenge for the incident on the water ride crossed his mind again and for a moment he wished that he was anywhere but in the bush, in the park, in the gathering dark. Mike pushed him in the back again, but gently this time.

"Sorry Joe," he whispered. "Come on, let's read the rest of that leaflet before it gets too dark."

Joe rolled over and smiled at Mike. Perhaps things would be alright after all.

It was then that Mike's phone rang. An electronic alarm call ringing out across the silence of the woods. The boys looked at each other.

"Didn't you just turn that off?" whispered Joe. Mike nodded. He fumbled in his pocket until he found it and then jabbed a finger turning it off before it could ring anymore. He peered at the screen and a frown creased his forehead.

"Who was it?" asked Joe.

Mike shook his head.

"Don't know. Don't recognise the number."

"How come it rang? Didn't you turn it off properly?"

Mike frowned harder and then shook his head.

"Dunno. Can't have. I thought I did. This should do it." And with that Mike took the battery out of the phone and put the two separate pieces in his pockets.

"Come on," Mike went on in a low, deep voice. "Let's get on with the reading while we've still got light."

Joe grunted his assent, but before he did so he took his own phone out and removed the battery. Better safe than sorry, he thought.

In the fading light the boys continued to read.

At first it seemed that the old man's words that had struck such terror into the Earl were nothing more than words. Days, weeks and months passed until the Earl became sure that all was well. He had, after all, made a pact with the Lord of Darkness himself, which he felt sure must protect him.

Although his middle son, Paul, had no knowledge of his father's deal with the devil, he had heard of the original curse, and so it was that when Paul arrived home on leave from the Royal

Flying Corp he found himself sitting in the plush red leather chairs in his father's study, a glass of finest brandy swilling in his hand.

The Earl confided to his son, in joking tones, that a local peasant, Edgar Trundle, had cursed him. The two men laughed at the absurdity of a curse in the modern age. Paul asked his father why the man would bother to impose a curse when one already existed. Albert muttered into his whisky but he had no answer.

However, his son's amusement at the tale assured the Earl that the old man's words were nothing more than bluster and superstition. Who was he to believe, the master of all the world's evil who had promised him salvation at the cost of his soul, or a semi-literate farm labourer whose brains were long past their best?

But still, there was something in those whispered words that stayed lodged in the Earl's memory, whispering to him as he lay awake at night.

And so came the morning of Paul's departure. It was a cold, clear December morning. The Earl rode down to the railway station with his son and waved him off. He was to fly back to France with one of the new Sopwith Scouts, or 'Pups' as the pilots called them, a delivery for the front line.

That night the Earl heard a hideous croaking drifting up from the lake. It lasted only ten minutes but it was enough to convince the Earl that it was the sound he had heard all those many times before. He prayed to God and he prayed to the Devil, but neither was listening. He convinced himself that it was a dream but he could not sleep that night and as the day dawned he dressed himself and steeled his tired soul for the telegram that he knew must surely come.

And come it did. The boy from the village post office cycled up the gravel drive to the Hall and delivered it into the Earl's weary hands.

Captain Paul de Tellier missing over channel Stop Aeroplane he was piloting believed to have ditched at sea Stop Search and rescue so far fruitless Stop Little hope of successful recovery Stop Commiserations Major General Flook-Smythe Stop End of message

The Earl was seen to screw up the telegram and throw it to the floor. He retired to his study where the servants heard him weeping. That night they reported the sounds of screaming and crying coming from the lake, and at dawn an exhausted Earl returned to the Hall, wet, shivering and almost half mad with grief. His butler rushed to his aid and the Earl confided in him the words that Edgar Trundle had spoken that day.

"The Devil giveth and the Devil taketh away. He may take your soul and give you freedom from one curse but he does nothing to protect you from another. I am here on Satan's business, my Lord, and if you will not give me my simple satisfaction then I will visit my forefathers' vengeance on you once again. To water, Sir, to water does the way of your doom lie, and may all whose blood be sourced in yours be damned to a watery grave. So lived the curse and so it lives again."

It was at this point that the Earl had thrust Trundle away from him as though he were plagued, but Trundle had one more departing message.

"Do not imagine you can do a deal with the Devil, Sir. He is the greatest of all tricksters and is not want to stick to his word, for his word is deception. We who follow him and honour him should surely know that Sir. Please do not doubt it."

And that was not the end of the matter. In July of the following year the croaking was once more heard and all who had heard it heard it with dread.

But the Earl was never to know what dreary news it foretold for that next morning when his butler brought in his breakfast he found his master propped up in bed with his throat cut and a razor in hand. A look of despair and fear was etched upon the old Earl's face for he knew where it was that he was going.

The news came later that week, Evelyn had died during the Battle of Ypres. Despite his father's insistence on his joining the army instead of the navy, the unfortunate Evelyn had indeed drowned. Badly wounded by a shell burst he had sought cover in a crater and had been unable to prevent himself sliding and sinking into the liquid mud at its bottom. He was found with just his hand protruding from the mire, a pistol still clutched in his fist, his finger curled uselessly around the trigger.

And so it was that the de Tellier fortune was left to Edward who was given leave to return from Southern Cameroon to settle the family's affairs. On his return home Edward was given a letter that had been found clutched in his father's hand, sealed with wax and creased in his death grip. The rolled paper was spattered with the rusty stains of his father's last blood.

Inside was a handwritten letter that advised Edward to take a wife in secrecy and allow her children to grow up with a new name, not that of de Tellier. Edward himself was to retain the family name but none of his descendents should be cursed with the name that had brought so much pain on its bearers. In this way Albert, 17th Earl of Culwick hoped to fool the curse by changing the name of his descendants. After Edward himself died he was to pass the hall on to another master whose family would reign over the de Tellier estates, the family that had brought down the wrath of Hell upon the de Tellier clan, the Trundle family.

The name that Edward was to bestow upon his future children was a strange one and he had to consult many an obscure reference book before he was able to discern its true meaning.

Werneria, the name of a genus of toad found only in Cameroon.

Both boys reached the end of the passage at the same time.

"But that means," whispered Mike. "With a name that weird, that means that I'm…"

"Yes," said Joe, his voice not especially quiet. "That you're a de Tellier."

"And Stevie," whispered Mike, awestruck. "Is the Earl of Culwick." He paused, taking it in, and then spoke again. "Just wait till I get home and tell him."

"Mmm," replied Joe, closing the booklet so that the rear cover was face up. There was a photo of the author on the back. "Actually Mike, he's not. You are. You share the same name as Stevie but Werneria's your dad's name and, you know, he wasn't actually Stevie's real dad. It's you. You're aristocracy mate. You're a bloody Earl. I suppose I'd better start bowing hadn't I."

Joe was trying to make light of the situation but he had realised the seriousness of the implications. He could tell by the look of Mike's face, fuzzy in the half-light, that he had too.

"But," said Mike, "that means I fall under the curse, the water curse."

"Only if you believe in that sort of nonsense," muttered Joe.

"And do you?"

Joe paused.

"No."

There was another pause.

"You know," said Mike, even quieter. "That meant that my dad fell under the curse too. And look what happened to him."

"Car crash," said Joe, dismissively, wanting to convince Mike, and to convince himself. "Could have happened to anyone."

Neither was convinced.

"It had just been raining, the surface of the road was wet," whispered Mike. "And you probably know, my dad had been drinking."

The silence stretched on and on. Joe could think of nothing to say. He leaned forward in the gloom to look more closely at the author photo on the back of the leaflet.

He sat up and took a gasping intake of breath.

"What is it?" Mike asked.

"The photo," Joe gasped. Neither of them was being quiet now, they weren't even attempting to. The shock of what they'd discovered had stunned them so much that they'd forgotten the need to take precautions.

"What about it?" Mike was nearly panicking, there was too much information coming too fast.

"It's the man, the man from the museum, the man who I was talking to. He wrote the booklet."

"So?"

"Look at his name."

Mike picked up the book and squinted at the photo. Slowly he sat up. He turned to look at Joe, his mouth open and eyes wide with disquiet. His mouth began to form words and then, as if catching up with his lips, whispered words came to Joe's ears, a name.

"Trundle. John Trundle."

Joe nodded. Suddenly, from out of the silence came the sound of footsteps on the path. They were moving fast, trying to be quiet, and there were voices, whispered, trying to conceal their presence. Joe grabbed Mike's arm and felt his whole body go tense and become motionless, felt his breathing cease like a small animal sensing a predator.

The sounds of the men drew rapidly nearer but lowered in volume as they seemed to sense the noise they were making. Beams of light from two torches bounced around in the rapidly darkening gloom and then the boys could make out the words of the men, the same voices as those who had passed earlier, almost comical in their attempt to stay quiet, their voices echoing among the trees in stage whispers.

161

"This is it, this is the spot.""

"Where's the trail then? It's supposed to be quite clear."

Joe's grip increased on Mike's arm until Mike had to prise his fingers off. There was the sound of feet moving and the beams swept the bushes.

"Got it!" called one of the men. "Over here." Then there was the sound of movement, large movement, big people crashing past foliage, heading along a narrow trail, their trail, heading directly for them.

Joe sat up.

"They're coming. They know we're here. We've got to go."

Mike didn't move.

"Quick," hissed Joe. "Before it's too late."

He gave Mike a shove and that was enough, he jerked into life as though from a trance. The boys grabbed their bags, fumbling, getting in each other's way. Mike headed for the hole that they'd come in by.

"No, not that one," whispered Joe.

The men were nearly at the top of the slope. If they were able to follow the trail in the dark without any problems then they'd be on top of them in ten seconds or less. Their only hope was that they'd pause and lose the track for a moment at the top of the slope.

"There's another gap, the one at the back, over here," Joe hissed.

Joe dived into the passage he had seen earlier, the badger or fox hole. He didn't know where it came out or even if it came out anywhere at all, all he knew was if they went out the other way then they'd get caught. Who knew what would happen then.

The second passage had a narrower entrance and the twigs and branches around it crashed and rattled as Joe struggled through. He hoped the men wouldn't hear him over the noise they were making themselves.

Suddenly he was out in the open, his legs pulling free of the bush. Joe rose to his feet and could hear Mike right behind, and then beyond that the sound of a man calling out, saying something, but Joe couldn't make out what it was. He glanced around but it was hard to make out anything definite, just lots more bushes, trees and other foliage. As soon as Mike began to emerge from the hole he grabbed him by the shoulders and hauled him to his feet.

"Run!" he hissed. "Follow me." And with that Joe turned and began to run into the wilderness that surrounded them, unsure of where he was going but heading as far away from the men as he possibly could.

It was almost as if his life depended on it.

Chapter 22

On the run

Joe ran like he had never run before. Although he was trying to move quietly he still heard himself crashing through the undergrowth and behind him heard, even louder, Mike following.

How could the men not have heard them? They must be right on their heels. Even Joe's own breathing ripping out of his lungs in hot panting strips seemed to scream their presence to their pursuers. He realised that with the noise they were making they might as well be carrying burning torches to alert the security guards to their whereabouts. What they needed was to find somewhere secluded to stop and lay low while their pursuers lost the scent.

Ahead of Joe in the gloom a large bush appeared. He darted sideways and then, finding no way through, ran along its curving length. Glancing back he could make out Mike's face, white against the dark blue of his clothing and the dark of the wood. Behind Mike he could see or hear nothing, but that wasn't enough to reassure him, he was certain that the men were still coming, something in his blood told him, something of the wild, a part of the animal that lies inside every human being waiting for times of danger and terror.

The overhanging branches and leaves blocked out the dieing light and cast an early night time over the gardens. It was growing increasingly difficult for Joe to see where he was going without tripping over fallen branches and dips in the ground.

He came to the end of the bush's branches and crashed through a gap between them and a wide tree trunk. He had just passed through to the other side when his feet flew out from under him and he felt himself sliding down a muddy bank. With a colossal force of will and with his tongue clamped between his teeth he was able to stop himself from calling out. With a crunch and a slight throbbing pain in his backside he came to rest on stony ground.

"Are you alright?" hissed Mike above him. He had seen what had happened to Joe and managed to avoid the drop.

"Yes. Come down quietly," Joe replied.

Joe picked himself up and as he did so a crunching sound came from under his feet. He looked down and then up and around and realised what the drop had been, he'd fallen into the cutting of the railway, the cutting they'd travelled down earlier that day on the train.

To his right the line curved away into darkness, but to the left a break in the tree cover let in enough moonlight to illuminate the wooden bridge that traversed the gorge they'd commented on earlier that day.

With a rustle on the slope and then a crash of gravel, Mike was down and next to him.

"Where are we?" he hissed.

"On the train track. If we keep going in that direction," said Joe pointing across the tracks to the opposite embankment, "we'll be at the edge of the lake in about twenty yards I reckon."

"But we don't want to do that do we? That can't be the best direction."

"No. Wait!"

They were silent, listening. Not too far away they could hear the men's voices and their hurried progress through the undergrowth. Because they were bigger the two men must have found the going harder, the gaps tighter to squeeze through. The crackle of the men's radio echoed amongst the trees.

"Bollocks!" spat Joe. "They're coming."

"Come on," said Mike. "Down the tracks."

The boys started running. It was hard, the sleepers were too close together to make walking on two at a time easy, but too far apart to make walking on three at a time easy. Within thirty yards they had both stumbled several times. They were also running further into a deep and steep sided cutting.

Mike hissed to Joe, "Stop. We've got to get out. If there are others coming to help and they come from both ends then we'll be trapped. We'll

166

definitely be trapped if it gets any deeper. We won't be able to get up the slope."

"You're right," nodded Joe, then he stopped, tilting his head as though he had heard something. "Listen!"

They listened. There was nothing, and then, further away, the sound of voices made its way to them.

They were far enough around the curve now to be unable to see the spot where they'd fallen into the cutting, but they were close enough to hear one of the men shout out in surprise and then swear in pain as he made the same mistake as they had, only harder.

Before the laughter was out of the boys' mouths something stopped it in their throats.

Mike's phone rang.

It was impossible, he had taken the battery out. Mike was so confused that he didn't react for a couple of rings.

"Do something," hissed Joe.

The swearing from down the railway line had stopped. The men had clearly heard the noise.

Mike ripped the phone from his pocket, glanced at the screen and then hurled it to the floor and stamped on it. The ringing stopped.

"Come on," said Joe and started scrambling up the side of the cutting that led to the lake. Mike followed.

The climb was steep enough to make them pause a moment at the top to catch their breath and it was during that brief pause that they heard it, from one side the sounds of feet running on gravel and on the other, the barking of dogs.

"Quick," said Mike. "The lake."

"The lake?" said Joe.

"Yeah, we can get there, and run through the water for a while, just at the edge, and then come out a bit further along. The dogs'll lose the scent. It'll take them some time to pick it up again if they ever do."

"Won't they follow us there?" said Joe.

"Why would they think we're going in that direction? It's got to be worth a try. We're knackered otherwise."

"Alright," said Joe. "You go first."

They slipped through more undergrowth, now almost silent in their determination to throw off their pursuers, but after a couple of minutes Mike stopped and gestured for Joe to come close. He leaned forward so he could whisper in Joe's ear.

"There was a message, on my phone, even though it didn't have any battery."

"What did it say?"

Joe stared at him, his eyes huge. He gulped and then spoke.

"Coming to get you."

The two boys stared at each other. Both knew it was impossible that the men could have their numbers. If, of course, they were men. Or, of course, if it was the men who had sent the message.

Without another word the boys began running again.

Chapter 23

The Water's Edge

Joe and Mike emerged from the undergrowth to find a full moon playing its cold blue light across the gently rippling surface of Lake Hobsdor. They stopped for a moment, panting, entranced by the beauty that lay before them. The surface of the water was inky black and the stars and moon stretched across it, wrinkled with the strokes of the wind.

Now that they were in the open and next to the water the boys could hear more of the night around them, the sounds of work going on in the park across the water, the sounds of an army of men and women who arrived after the fun-seekers had gone home, to clean up their mess, to check the safety of the rides, to get it ready for the next day, an army of the unseen.

And then they could hear the dogs again.

"Come on," whispered Mike.

The boys made their way down to the water. They had to pick their way gingerly as the ground was rocky and uneven. They were still a good twenty feet away and it took them a couple of minutes before they were actually at the water's edge. Any second Joe expected to hear a voice calling 'STOP!' But nothing came.

As they got to the water Joe grabbed Mike by the shoulder. He held his finger to his lips and looked back at the tree line. The boys waited. There was no sound. The men must still be in the cutting. The barking of the dogs was faint yet.

"We're really exposed here," said Joe. "If someone comes out of the bushes they'll see us straight away. We've got to get moving and find some cover."

Mike nodded.

"Which way do you think is best?"

They both looked each way and then decided at the same time.

"Right," they both said and laughed at the coincidence, slightly hysterical with the tension.

Without speaking they sat on the rocks and pulled off their trainers and socks, shoving the socks inside.

"What do you think was going on with my phone?" asked Mike.

"Don't know," replied Joe. "Don't think about it."

They were silent for a moment as they finished their task.

"Ready?" said Mike, standing up, his black Adidas dangling from his right hand. Joe nodded. Mike looked at him.

"You think it'll be okay don't you? You know, the water, what with the curse and everything?"

Joe couldn't meet his eye.

"Yeah, of course it will you fanny. Be careful not to splash."

They waded in on the smooth slimy pebbles for about three feet. The water wasn't as cold as they'd expected and, in fact, was quite refreshing on their hot sweaty feet. It came halfway up their shins and allowed them to slide their legs through the water rather than lift them out and so prevented them from making too much noise as they headed towards the small jutting headland that lay thirty yards to their right.

Mike was behind Joe and getting impatient. Joe was being too cautious, moving too slowly. The sound of the dogs was getting louder and he was pretty sure that he'd heard the fuzzing of the radio.

"Hurry, they'll be coming out of the woods any minute."

"I'm going as fast as I can," hissed Joe. "I can't see where I'm putting my feet. If I fall over then everybody in ten miles is going to hear."

"Shut up and go faster."

At that moment Joe's phone rang.

"Kill it! Kill it!" hissed Mike.

"It's off, it shouldn't be ringing," Joe replied through panicky gritted teeth. He took out the phone and without looking at the screen pulled back his arm and hurled it as far as he could out into the lake. As it arched through the air its ring made a wobbling sound and then it hit the surface some thirty feet away with a tiny splash. The ring continued, muted for a couple of seconds, and then died.

"What the bloody hell is going on?" whispered Joe.

"Keep on moving, keep on moving," urged Mike. "They'll definitely be coming now."

They sloshed onwards, glancing behind them every so often to see if their pursuers had appeared. As soon as they did the boys would surely be spotted if they were still in the water.

They were ten feet from the shore when Joe cried out, a broken scream of revulsion. He'd tried to stifle it, smother the cry, but what he had felt had been too repulsive.

"What is it?" hissed Mike, his scalp crawling with horror.

"Nothing," said Joe through gritted teeth. "Something just touched my leg. It must have been an eel or a fish. Let's get out of here."

But he knew that it wasn't a fish or an eel. Whatever it was had been so thickly coated with slime that he had felt his leg go *into* whatever it had been, sink and slide into it, and yet it had moved, had been alive.

He started staggering through the water, not caring that he was making so much noise. He had to get out of the lake. Panic was building in him like an unstoppable tide and he was worried that if he didn't escape the chilly clutches of the lake then it might overtake him, freeze him into a state of petrified inaction.

He heard Mike coming after him, running as well. Whatever it was that had touched Joe in the darkness had been so cold and loathsome, so filled with dynamic and repulsive life that it had made his fear of capture dissolve. All he wanted was to be out of the water.

Joe had almost reached the shoreline when he realised that he couldn't hear Mike splashing behind him anymore. He turned, his feet still up to their ankles in the water.

Looking back he saw that for some reason Mike had stopped and had turned to face the middle of the lake. He was bending slightly, peering into the darkness.

"Joe," he called in a whisper without turning around. "Come and look at this."

"What is it?" Joe couldn't understand. What was Mike doing? Just seconds before they'd been running in a blind panic and now he was entranced by something in the water.

"I don't know," Mike said. "I don't know."

Despite his fear, there was something in Mike's voice that made Joe take a couple of steps back into the lake towards him.

And then he saw it.

Them.

Lying somewhere under the surface, perhaps ten yards away from Mike were two huge, glowing yellow objects. Transfixed, Joe took another step towards them. The ripples on the surface of the water made it hard to figure out what shape the objects were, but they must have been big, as big as…Joe couldn't think what, and then it came to him, rugby balls.

Mike took another step towards the lights.

"Don't do that Mike," said Joe, not even trying to keep his voice low anymore. "Come back."

"No," said Mike, waving the idea away with a dismissive hand, not bothering to turn to look back at Joe. He was fixed on the lights, enraptured.

Joe realised that Mike was no longer holding his trainers in his hands. Somewhere he must have dropped them into the lake, both of them.

"It's fine, Joe," said Mike, his voice had a strange ecstatic quality. "They're beautiful, so beautiful. What can they be? The way they glow, they must be gold or something."

And then the wind dropped, and as the wind dropped, so did the ripples in the water and it became as still and as true as a looking glass.

Joe realised what the lights were and he lost control of his bladder.

The lights were eyes. Huge eyes devoid of feeling, and they were staring at Mike.

Joe managed to get his friend's name out in a strangled warning but it was too late. Joe never knew if Mike had seen what he had seen. He never knew if Mike had realised what was in front of him, what the lights were.

In a sudden explosion the eyes leaped from the water, an enormous darkness obscuring the stars. Mike never had a chance to make a sound before he disappeared forever into that huge tooth lined mouth of infinite and unending darkness.

And then as soon as it had exploded from the water it was gone and the water folded neatly back into its smoothly rippled, unbroken surface, only the light pitter patter of water droplets falling back into the lake.

Joe stood, gently rocking on his heels in the shallow water, his eyes wide and staring unseeing into the distance. His mind raced desperately to comprehend what it was that he had just seen but the scramble of confusion and fear was too much and a dark veil began to fall over Joe's world. Something deep within his mind snapped with a ping that was audible only to Joe and was the last thing he was aware of as consciousness left him and his legs collapsed. He crumpled in a faint, face first into the lake.

As the water settled back into its quiet rhythmic lapping, a figure detached itself from the darkness of the woods and made its way into the lake. John Trundle, the old man from the museum, the watcher, carried Joe's limp and dripping body from the water and laid it gently on the grass. Standing, the old man gazed down at the unconscious boy before turning and disappearing back into the darkness from which he had come.

Chapter 23

Aftermath

Joe was found twenty minutes later by the two men who had been chasing him and Mike. At first they were delighted to have caught someone, it had never been done before and they were hoping to get a bonus in their paycheque. When they saw the state Joe was in, however, they were not quite so happy, realising they might soon have a corpse on their hands if they weren't careful.

The bigger of the two men picked him up and began walking back to the centre of the park as quickly and carefully as he could while the other man radioed for help on the walkie talkie, hurrying along behind his colleague.

An ambulance was called and Joe was taken to hospital where his condition was made stable. But he didn't wake up. The police were called but were unable to find out who Joe was and it was not until the following morning when both Joe and Mike's bags were found washed up on the shore of Lake Hobsdor that it became clear who they were. Neither boy's parents had reported them missing as each believed their boys to be with the other's parents on a supervised trip away. How they wished they had checked this when the police officers arrived on their doorsteps to deliver the bad news.

Joe remained in a coma and although police divers searched Lake Hobsdor nothing more was found of Mike apart from one of his black Adidas trainers, washed up on the shoreline.

After a fortnight Joe woke up but he was unable to help the police or anyone else. All Joe could do was stare blankly from his bed, his eyes focussed on something far away, something terrible, something of which he could never ever speak. And so he remained, silent and uncommunicative for the next ten years.

Six months after Mike's disappearance, during the winter period when the park was closed, a park employee who was helping resurface the coach park made a peculiar discovery. Chained to a metal fence were two very rusty bicycles.

Chapter 24

Epilogue: Ten Years After

The night was still and very dark, a lonely darkness untainted by street lamps or shop lights. Nothing moved or made a sound, it was as though the creatures of the night knew something strange was afoot and were holding their breath. Through skeletal trees and scudding clouds the cold blue of the winter moon cast brittle shadows. Snaking through the loamy soil, a thin stream trickled and gurgled in the silence. A narrow path ran along the edge of the water, a flattened line of grass rarely trodden, but in the wetness of the soil were footprints leading upstream. They followed the water until the woodland gave way, the trees stopping abruptly in the face of a wall that loomed as tall as a tower block, filling the valley through which the river wound.

From a concrete-lined sluice near the base of the wall a steady flow of water emerged, falling into a pool where it bubbled and foamed before overflowing and becoming the stream. Beyond the wall hundreds of thousands of gallons of murky water hung in the dammed valley, dark depths, weed strewn and treacherous, pressing against the obstruction.

From the sluice came scraping sounds. A man emerged from the round opening, soaking wet and breathing hard. He dangled his legs over the edge and then pushed himself off, landing with a splash in the pool. In his left hand he held a reel of cable which trailed back into the darkness. Reaching up to the outer rim of the sluice he found a small black plastic box with a switch on its surface. Carefully he attached the cable in his hand to an opening in the back of the box.

The man was dressed in black combat trousers, a black polo neck and army boots. On his back he wore a dark, waterproof knapsack. His clothes shone in the moonlight where the water had soaked in, clinging to his thin muscular body.

Pausing for a moment he looked to the star scattered sky. A section was obscured by a strip of blackness, unmarked by the glittering pin pricks, a wooden bridge supported at either end by tall towers. The valley that the bridge traversed was narrow, no more than forty feet wide, but it had steep sides. It would have been beautiful if it had not been amputated, blocked by the huge dam from which the man had climbed.

He splashed through the pool, unconcerned by the noise, and stepped onto the bank. He settled, took one look up at the wall, and then flicked the switch.

He had been waiting a long time for this moment. He had known that he must do something and in the long hours in the communal hall he had developed a plan. Despite the noise and suffering of those around he had remained in silence, his mind working, fathoming, meticulously plotting. After many years the many petalled flower of his plan had begun to bloom, every part in its perfect place, slowly opening. The nurses had noticed the change, he had never smiled before. It was a moment he would always remember, a beautiful moment of clarity as he'd gazed onto the lawns, the sound of a television game show blaring behind him.

That evening he had packed and left. There was no need to escape, he was not a prisoner, he was no danger to himself or anybody else. Before the incident at the theme park he had been a happy and outgoing boy, or so they said.

He had shaved his hair in the bathroom mirror and left in the dead of night. He knew there would have been questions otherwise and he knew he had no answers.

His parents still came and visited, though less frequently than in the early days. Mike's mother had come a few times at the beginning, sometimes sober, sometimes not, always begging for answers, answers he couldn't give.

Joe's mother had told him that Mike's mum gave up alcohol a month after Mike's disappearance, but by that point she had stopped visiting so Joe never saw the new 'clean' Mrs Werneria.

At least one good thing had come out of it, Joe thought.

On one of her visits, soon after Mike's disappearance, Joe's mother had told him that Mike's mum was pregnant. It wasn't the new bloke, the one from the pub who no one really approved of, the one who was too young. The young bloke wouldn't say why it couldn't have been him, but he knew it couldn't. He left Mrs Werneria, he thought she'd been cheating, but she hadn't. She'd been pregnant all along. It turned out that it was Mike's dad who was the father. Dead Mr Werneria. Mike's mum's periods were a bit mixed up due to her drinking and she hadn't noticed she was pregnant for the first four months. When she gave up alcohol, her mind and body got straightened out and she realised what was up with her.

Joe's face hadn't even flickered in response to the news.

When the baby was born Joe's mum came in and told him. It was a little boy and everything was fine with it. They'd been worried because of all the drinking she'd done earlier in the pregnancy.

A little baby de Tellier boy.

Everything was fine. Except it wasn't of course. His name was Thomas.

Joe had blinked and turned to look at his mother. For a moment she thought he might say something, a flame of hope rising in her heart, but he remained silent.

Inside his head though, Joe was awake in every possible way, thinking, scheming, dedicated to saving that newborn child from a destiny of disaster, a fate that was no more its own fault than its eye or hair or skin colour had been.

Joe knew what he had to do but not how to do it. But he knew he had time, time and solitude, alone on the ward. For the next ten years he plotted and planned. And then he was ready.

Crouching in a pool of cold water, soaked to the skin, Joe remembered the moment he'd heard the news about baby Thomas. Now Thomas wasn't much younger than when Mike had been killed. He was here to avenge his friend and lift the age old curse once and for all. He was here to save Mike's brother.

Taking a deep breath Joe flicked the switch.

There was a huge rumble followed by a noise that might have been a deep throated roar of anger. The earth seemed to jolt and shake and there was a burst of dust from the hole followed by a gout of water. Then, quite suddenly, it settled back into its previous gurgle.

It was as though nothing had happened.

The man remained motionless. From deep within the wall came a tearing sound, slow and agonised. A bulge appeared high on the face of the dam, the stonework crazing and cracking.

Joe scrambled to his feet and started to run.

He was half way up the steep slope that led to the top of the valley, almost underneath the wooden viaduct, when the green skin of the bulging dam ripped apart with a belching roar, scattering clods of earth and chunks of concrete as it exploded with the pressure of hundreds of tons of water. The torrent that followed was a boiling wall of white water that filled the empty space of the valley in seconds. The roar that filled the air seemed to be all around him. A mountain of liquid ripped the gantries of the bridge away and the structure seemed to explode as it collapsed. Chunks of wood cascaded down around Joe's head. A sleeper nearly decapitated him, the jagged piece of wood thumping into the ground. Joe struggled onwards, the water at his heels. He knew that to slip or to pause meant to be carried off to certain death, drowned or dashed against rocks.

He made it to the summit, rolled over and struggled, panting to his feet. The water had stopped rising five feet below the top of the gorge and Joe realised he had been within inches of death.

The water was sliding out of the rip in the wall like the back of some enormous serpent. To his left he could see the two rails that had passed over the bridge, now without their sleepers but still sagging across the rushing abyss.

Joe looked out across the surface of the lake. The moon reflected on the water as it moved slowly towards the rent in the wall, and then, as it neared the rip, faster and faster. Watching the edge of the lake where water met land, Joe could see the levels were falling. Stone, draped in green weed was being revealed and Joe saw flapping movements where only minutes before had been water. He realised he was watching fish in their death throes and for a moment he felt regret.

Then he remembered why he had done what he had and the evil that would die with the waters that flowed from his act of destruction.

Despite the danger of the police arriving, and if not the police, the park security, Joe remained where he was. He had run once before. This time he would remain. This he must see.

The lake continued to drain and it was not long before a broken finger of jagged masonry appeared in the swirling waters. It was the church tower, still standing after all these years. Slowly, bit by bit, it revealed itself, ruined and half standing, like a leper lowering her veil.

Then came the remains of the cottages, their roofs long gone but the walls mostly standing.

The lake was almost drained now and all that remained was the water that swilled past the walls of the buildings in the bottom of this long forsaken valley, a valley that was seeing moonlight for the first time in over two hundred years, moonlight not filtered through fifty feet of water.

The waters rushed around the buildings, the walls, the windows, the door frames, and across and down the silt coated roads where once feet and hooves and wheels had travelled. At last the village could breathe again.

Although Joe cold not see from where he stood, within the dark remains of the long abandoned houses, houses that had once echoed with laughter and conversation, terrible relics were being revealed. In one was a wetsuit and oxygen canister entangled in weeds. Nearby lay a single frogman's flipper and a glass face mask green with algae. Within the wetsuit a man's bones were still snugly enshrouded.

In another house on the opposite side of the main street lay two sets of bones, intermingled and mixed for all time as though they had settled in a last desperate embrace. One skeleton was much smaller than the other, its little skull lying next to another larger, adult sized skull, a skull that had belonged to his nurse who had never left him, never let him go, even at the last as their bodies had slowly drifted down through the depths and gently settled in the silt where they had lain entwined and undisturbed.

As the waters fell still further Joe's eyes were drawn to a glowing light in the middle of the village not far from the teetering remains of the church spire. It was circular and the glow that came from it was a deep angry red, a light that emanated with a horrible strength and vitality. It must be the well, Joe thought, where the villagers had sunk their buckets to draw up water from deep in the earth.

And then, in the light of the moon that bathed the broken remains of the village, Joe saw movement, a horrible flopping movement of something huge and cumbersome. It heaved and slumped towards the circle of red light and then, with a faint, slapping noise, it cast itself into the centre of the circle. There was a distant sound of sizzling and slowly the red light dwindled and faded until finally it died and the circle was gone.

Just as Joe heard the sounds of heavy footsteps approaching from behind he uttered the first words he had spoken in ten long years.

"It's over."

The old man who had been watching from the edge of the trees smiled and disappeared into the darkness.

Two pairs of strong hands seized Joe by the shoulders and pulled his hands behind his back.

Down in the new valley, outside the doorway of a ruined cottage in the deep brown mud, lay another skull, a not quite fully grown skull. The skull was polished and made white by the movement of the strange currents that had so recently swirled in these depths. It had not been there long, no more than ten years.

It was the skull of Michael Werneria, 22nd Earl of Culwick.

Printed in Great Britain
by Amazon